Exit Strategy

Barbara Winkes

ISBN: 978-1-0696671-5-1

For D.

Chapter One

Joanna caught the last few minutes of Rue's training when she went to get her for dinner. It was the evening before their first vacation day. Rue wasn't going to miss one session, kickboxing or therapy.

As she leaned against the far wall, studying her, Joanna had to admit she was enjoying the sight, a pleasure tinged with guilt as she knew this sport wasn't a random choice for Rue. Here on the island, they were safe—in the physical sense. The mind could play tricks at times, and Rue had countered them with new habits.

When Rue joined her on the floor, she was drenched in sweat, wisps of damp hair sticking to her face.

"Don't come too close," she warned. "Let me take a quick shower before we go?"

"Sure. I'll be here."

Rue looked her up and down, a smile tugging at the corners of her mouth, though she didn't comment.

"What?"

"Nothing. I'm just surprised, that's all. See you in a bit." She headed for the showers before Joanna could ask if the surprise was a good one. Judging from Rue's appreciative gaze, she assumed it to be. She hadn't worn a dress in years, but the long-skirted sundress, a flower pattern on black, seemed appropriate for the surroundings and the occasion. She, too, had adopted a few new habits.

"Hey, Joanna," Rue's trainer Zach greeted her. Everyone working at the inn knew each other by name. That, too, was safe, because they understood discretion, asking for it, and providing it.

"Hey. How is she doing?" She might be hovering and crossing lines with this question, but Joanna couldn't take Rue's presence lightly. She had to do everything in her power to make it worthwhile, foresee potential obstacles.

"She's got a lot of rage," he said thoughtfully. "I think this is a good way for her to channel it."

Joanna nodded. This came as no surprise to her. Rue had good reasons for her anger, but every once in a while, Joanna needed to make sure it was all because of the serial killer who had kidnapped her, and not because of the way her life had been uprooted afterwards. The latter had been her choice. She had chosen to be with Joanna. Again, nothing to take lightly.

"If you're done chatting, let's get out of here. I'm starving," Rue declared. She had dressed in shorts and a blouse and toweled off her hair. It wouldn't take long to dry in the local temperature.

"Have a great evening," Zach told her. "I'll see you Thursday?"

"You bet."

Outside the building, Rue stopped cold when she realized Joanna had brought the car.

"We're going somewhere? Don't tell me I missed an anniversary."

"No, don't worry." This kind of surprises meant stress. Joanna hurried to explain. "It's the beginning of our vacation. I didn't feel like going to the inn. Is that okay with you?"

"Yes. Of course."

She could sense Rue relax next to her.

"Good. I thought we deserved something special."

What they thought they deserved, and got, it could be a tricky question at times.

"It's a great idea." Rue leaned in to kiss her softly. "What did you have in mind?"

"We said we might try the seafood restaurant near the pier."

"Can we afford it?"

"Sure we can. We both have jobs." In the beginning, Joanna had worried that both their jobs might be subject to some artificial inflation. It turned out that there was enough for them to do at the inn to justify full-time employment that paid for their life here. Joanna helped out wherever she was needed, and she enjoyed the flexible work a lot more than she could have imagined. Rue, who had been a personal assistant to Joanna's father in another life, had quickly worked her way into the inn's management. The house cost them next to nothing.

"Okay. Let's do it."

The restaurant turned out to be an excellent choice. They sat by the window, watching the sunset and then the moon rising in the darkened sky.

Rue had a glass of white wine. Joanna stuck to water. Back in the city, she had smoked and drunk too much, sometimes even when her life wasn't spiraling out of control. She was down to a drink or two on the weekend. Distance was a lifesaver.

"I love it," Rue said. "I mean, the inn has great people, but this is different."

Joanna could only agree. The romantic atmosphere had her both wistful and excited. Strange to think that save for some highly traumatic events, they wouldn't be here, together. A moment like this, it was hard not to imagine proposing to Rue. It was harder to imagine that anything could bring them closer together than those shared experiences.

"It's nice. We should come another time at least."

"Yes, but it's our vacation. Let's not plan too much."

"We won't. I promise."

At times, Joanna would strain to listen to every minute change in tone, to determine every little flicker of mood. But there were moments like this when she was able to abandon her frantic analysis and enjoy the presence of the woman who had left everything behind, for her. Well, perhaps not just for Joanna. Rue appreciated the geographical and psychological distance to certain incidents as well.

After the meal, they walked along the pier, with an ice cream cone for dessert. After all these months, Joanna had lost the fear that someday, a tourist could recognize her, and an avalanche of trouble would follow for both of them. It appeared that the authorities back in the city didn't want her that badly. A cruel, sadistic man was dead.

If her involvement was curious and questionable, they hadn't wasted much time finding her. That meant Theo and Vanessa were fine, and she didn't need to worry about anything.

These days, her focus was on making sure Rue was okay, blissful distance, and the day-to-day job.

She still wondered when it would be the right time to say the words. She'd wait. Joanna wanted to do everything perfectly. She'd need a ring—and wear something that would make it easier to get down on one knee.

"What are you thinking?" Rue asked.

"That I'm so happy you're here," Joanna said, pulling her close for a kiss.

Rue was happy, too. At least that was the most plausible explanation. They celebrated the start of their vacation some more, making love and enjoying another night without bad dreams. It might be the longest stretch since they started their life together.

In the morning, Joanna stole out of bed and prepared coffee. With her cup, she returned to the bedroom, smiling at Rue, who was still fast asleep and tangled in the covers.

Peace. It wasn't something that had come easily to either of them, but damn, they had earned it. Every moment of it.

She went to set the table on the small terrace. One of the reasons Joanna loved this house was that there was little chance for anyone to surprise them. Every car had to come up the hill, in plain sight. They didn't have visitors, and the only unexpected arrival had been Rue's...but it was always better to be safe than sorry.

They were close enough to the inn to walk on foot, but not close enough to be disturbed by anyone. Former Internal Affairs Inspector Vanessa Young had found the perfect solution for them. Irony, or poetic justice, Joanna wasn't always sure, not that it mattered anymore.

In her old life, she'd never taken the time to listen to birds sing. She didn't think there was time, back then, when she was chasing murderers, then ghosts, and her own demons. Joanna was done chasing. She was home.

As if on cue, Rue arrived on the terrace, hiding a yawn behind her hand.

"I see my timing is perfect. You're all done. Sorry about that."

"That's okay. You needed the rest, I assume."

Rue's smile told her she'd taken the insinuation as intended.

"I did. Wow. It's kind of extreme, everything that needed to happen for me to take a vacation."

"I'm sorry my old man was such a horrible boss." Joanna wasn't sorry at all that Rue had found a way to leave the company. At the inn, everyone knew that they were a couple, and no one batted an eye.

"Well, look who's got the last laugh."

"You took a pretty big pay cut." Sometimes she had to stoke things, just a little, to make sure they were still on the same page. Joanna could do so safely, because Rue knew her patterns.

"And I get to live and work in a paradise. With you. Every once in a while, I'm petty enough to wish he could see that." Rue took a sip of coffee and closed her eyes in bliss. "I know I say this almost every morning, but it never tasted this good in the city."

Joanna saw no reason to argue with Rue on the subject of her father. No matter what they achieved, happiness, careers, the perfect life—Lawrence would always find fault with one issue in particular. But she didn't have to care, not anymore.

The island taught her every day what she'd managed, and what she might still be longing for, but Rue was right. They had made it this far, against odds stacked high against them.

Peace. Paradise. Joanna might be the kind of person afraid of trusting something too good to be true, but she couldn't deny the facts.

"Everything tastes better," she agreed, meaning it in a general sense. Rue's blush made her smile.

This was their version of the good life.

❧

They spent the day on the beach, had a picnic for a late lunch and came home to wash off the sand and sunscreen before going to dinner at the inn. In the beginning, Joanna had accepted the owner's offer mostly for practicality. Now that Rue was living with her, they took turns driving to town for groceries and ate at the inn's restaurant less often.

Rue was still in the bathroom when Joanna sat down at the piano that had come with the house as the last owners didn't want to move it.

She wasn't that great at it, hadn't practiced in a long time. The piano lessons she'd gotten as a young girl were among the few things for which she was still grateful to her parents. Joanna's mother had left when she was ten years old, her father had decided she no longer deserved his support when he found out she was dating a girl in college.

Things hadn't always been so disappointing. The piano called to her, even though she abandoned the melody the moment Rue returned from the bathroom.

"That was nice," she said. "You never play when I'm in the room."

"I might, someday." Joanna laughed as she got up. "Believe me, for now, I'm doing you a favor. You're ready to go?"

"I am. I think I'll need to ask Zach for some extra sessions. It seems like all we do is eat and lounge on the beach."

"That's not all we've done."

"I stand corrected. But now I'm hungry. Let's go."

Since neither of them had to drive tonight, Joanna had a beer as while Rue sipped on a colorful cocktail. It reminded her of how they'd first met, a chance encounter in a dingy bar, a place where Joanna had often hung out with Vanessa and on occasion made bad decisions. Rue's date had stood her up.

"You are getting lost in the what-if again," Rue whispered.

"Am I that transparent?"

"It might be that I had too much therapy, but yes, you are. Who knows what might have happened? I might have run into some bad people and have no one coming for me. But you did. And I want to be here. You hear me?"

"I hear you," Joanna said, reaching out to take her hand.

"You'll play for me sometime?" They both laughed.

"I know what you're doing, but no, I'm not ready. Let me practice a few more weeks...or months."

Joanna found Rue's pout as sexy as it was adorable. She was about to add something when Denise, the inn's owner, stopped at their table.

"Good evening, ladies. I hope everything is to your satisfaction?"

"What is it?" Joanna asked.

"What do you mean? You're my guests tonight, so I hope you have everything you need to leave a good review."

"And?"

Denise made a face. "You got me. I'm so sorry. I know you're on vacation, but is there any chance you could check on the air conditioning in 213 later? If it's something more severe, I can call in the technician first thing in the morning, but I still harbor the hope that it's something you might be able to fix."

"No problem. Let me finish my plate, and I can go take a look? We wanted to hang out here a bit longer anyway."

"That would be great, thank you so much."

"I'll let you know what I find, if anything."

Turning back to Rue, Joanna found her expression impassive.

"You're okay with that, right? It won't take long. I'll come find you in the bar."

"Okay." Rue sighed. In the first couple of weeks, they had barely spent a moment apart, even seen each other at work a lot, but that wasn't the case any longer. Rue went by herself to training and therapy, and to the grocery store. Her work hours didn't always overlap with Joanna's.

"Sure?"

"I said it was okay. I'm a bit disappointed," she continued after a small pause. "It's only the first day, and they already find something for you to do."

"We owe Denise a great deal."

"You're right," Rue acknowledged. "It's probably nothing big."

"I'll be quick," Joanna promised. "The sooner I do this, the sooner we can forget about it."

"Let's hope."

"Come on. We'll have all night—and another ten days." Joanna leaned closer and whispered, "And we don't have to come back here."

That earned her a small smile from Rue, a success in her book.

Chapter Two

A man in his late thirties or early forties greeted her in 213. Joanna couldn't help noticing the dresses spread out on the bed.

"My wife is in the bathroom," he said. "I'd be happy if you could do this quick."

"Don't worry, I'll just take a look. If there's nothing I can do, you could get another room."

"We'll live with it for one night if we must," he grumbled. "That doesn't bode well for our time here."

"I'm really sorry, sir." Joanna thought about Denise's joke regarding reviews. She hoped she could keep this guest from leaving a bad one anywhere. She checked the air conditioning, aware of the man hovering over her. It made her antsy and irritated, nothing she could let show. To her relief, she could diagnose the problem pretty much right away: Someone had turned the air conditioning all the way down and taken out the plug. The system was fairly new.

"Excuse me, sir, could you give me some space here?" She was surprised at the flash of anger on his face. He composed himself quickly and stepped away.

"Of course."

"Thank you."

Perhaps she should cut him some slack. They might be jet lagged, or on their honeymoon. In any case this wasn't a welcome distraction for anyone, and Joanna would have preferred to stay with Rue. After plugging in the air conditioning and turning it to mid-level, she waited for the soft sound to come on.

"This should be working now," she said. Her gaze went to the still closed bathroom door.

He moved to block it, or perhaps it was just her impression. If anyone understood the need for privacy, it was Joanna.

The man didn't thank or tip her. She didn't envy his wife. At least she could go back to Rue.

As they had agreed on, Rue was waiting for her at the bar, at a corner table where no one would bother her. Come to think of it, everyone on this island took privacy seriously.

"Hey. That wasn't too long, was it?"

"True." Rue got up to pull her into a close embrace. "You fixed things?"

"If you can call it that. I plugged the thing and turned it on."

"The maid forgot?"

"I don't know, but as far as I know we are full, and it's pretty much always on."

"Well, it's not your problem anymore. Let's celebrate that."

She waved to the waiter, and Joanna willed herself to forget the impolite man. It wasn't like she depended on his tip, and plenty of guests were more appreciative. This time, they both went with a cocktail. After all, their home and bed were only a short walk away.

Joanna woke with a start, unable to determine why. Rue was sleeping peacefully, and she couldn't remember any nightmares.

She sat up in bed, listening for any sounds that might be out of place, but there was nothing but her own rapid heartbeat, calming as she found nothing to be concerned about.

She left the bed to get some water from the fridge and looked out of the window. The road leading up the hill to their home was dark and silent. Sometimes, the wind carried over faint sounds from the inn, but they faded into the background. It was still early in their vacation. No reason to worry about anything. Rue had a therapy session the next day, and they'd spend the day in town afterwards. Lunch, window shopping...They didn't need much for a comfortable lifestyle.

Joanna lay back down, but she couldn't fall asleep. Something bothered her...Something about the man in 213. Given her history, she might be, and probably was, paranoid. Someone had forgotten to plug in the air conditioning. It was no longer her problem.

"What is it?" Rue asked, startling her despite the soft tone.

"Nothing. Go back to sleep."

"Talk to me. Please."

"I don't know what to tell you. Too much of that sweet cocktail maybe?"

"Did Vanessa ever offer you to get therapy here?"

Joanna thought back to the moment she'd arrived on the island, when Vanessa's contact had laid out her options to her.

"I wasn't kidnapped," she said.

"Not really the point. You've been through a lot. Maybe you'd like to talk to someone...Other than me, that is."

"I'm fine. That's not it." She suppressed a sigh, not wanting to worry Rue. They didn't mingle with the guests, but even so it was easy to tell that some came with secrets, people who came together that didn't want anyone to know they were together. The occasional businessman with a woman that wasn't his wife—or with another man. It happened, and Joanna considered herself far from being able to judge anyone. This was the first time that her thoughts lingered, and this moment, she realized why.

The whole time she'd been in the room, there was absolutely no sound from the bathroom. No running water, no sounds of a hairdryer, or anyone moving in there. Total quiet.

It didn't mean something nefarious was going on, but it was strange.

"The guy was pretty weird, hovering, and he wanted me to get out quickly. Didn't even give me a tip."

"So, he's a jerk, or he just wanted to be alone with his wife," Rue suggested. "That keeps you up?"

When Joanna didn't answer, she continued, "You found him suspicious?"

Joanna realized that she was scaring her.

"Petty more than anything. Like I said, it was probably the cocktail."

She had left a message for Denise, but was going to follow up with her, just in case. She wanted to know who the silent woman was, if only for her own peace of mind.

⁂

After they had breakfast together, Joanna drove Rue to town for her appointment. She parked next to the building, and after Rue had gone in, called Denise.

"I got your message, thank you so much," Denise said. "They made it sound urgent."

"Really? He didn't seem happy to see me. Besides, they could have easily fixed it themselves."

"Well, the woman said they needed someone right away."

"Did you see them? What's your impression?"

Denise was silent, as if trying to understand why Joanna was asking these questions.

"Husband and wife on their honeymoon. I've never seen either of them here before. Why do you ask?" Now that the question was out in the open, Joanna had to come up with something other than her intuition.

"He was a bit strange. Not a peep from the wife. She had some clothes laid out on the bed, but I didn't see her."

"You don't usually ask questions about our guests."

Joanna knew that Denise had a general idea about her story. She had to, in order to provide all the conditions Vanessa's contact had asked for. Did it matter? Joanna had been a cop once. The silence of women worried her. It wasn't something she could turn off.

"And I shouldn't start. I'm sorry about that. If that's all, I'll see you after the vacation."

She'd hoped that Denise would be the one to let her off the hook, her conscience and perhaps misplaced guilt and worries. Joanna's hope had been premature.

"The bride's quite young, but nothing we haven't seen here before. I saw him at the bar a couple of times and thought it was strange, but maybe she just wanted some time to herself." She sounded worried. Sometimes, Joanna had that effect on people, but she assumed this wasn't the first time Denise had doubts about the couple.

"If there's anything out of the ordinary, I'll let you know. You do the same?"

"And you will do what?"

"I don't know. Unfortunately, there are plenty of neglected wives. Being a jerk isn't a crime."

"Yeah, I hope there isn't more to it. Let's keep in touch. Thank you."

When Joanna ended the call, she realized it was still early into Rue's session. She got out of the car to walk further on main street, along souvenir shops and restaurants, one of which they'd choose for lunch later. So much for their quiet, relaxed vacation. It didn't help that Denise, too, had observed behavior that seemed out of place for a loving couple.

Should they intervene? Could they? How? Joanna had gone from a by-the-book cop to a vigilante and from there to...She wasn't sure what term to use. Her job had been to fix one specific item. She was once again lost in the what if, as Rue called it.

Almost time to meet her. Definitely time to snap out of it.

⁂

Rue was already sitting in one of the chairs in the lobby, waving to Joanna when she entered the building. Ten minutes early. She had a smile on her face. This was a good moment to remind herself that she wasn't responsible for everyone's happiness. Contributing whatever she could to Rue's, and working on her own, was what mattered.

"How was it?" Joanna asked as she hugged her. By the time Rue had arrived on the island, she had already begun the task of working through the trauma. That task, Joanna was aware, was in no way done, even though she was able to work, spend time by herself, and sleep without night terrors most nights.

"Low-key. Focus on safe space, rest, and relaxation."

"Sounds like a good idea." Was the woman in 213 safe? Why couldn't she let it go?

"It is. I'm tempted to try those exercises on you." They walked along the same row of restaurants and shops. Rue stopped to look at a scarf.

"Maybe that's a good idea too."

"You couldn't fall asleep."

At a moment's notice, Joanna decided not to tell her about the phone call with Denise. She didn't want to make Rue think something, someone had invaded paradise, this space where they could work through past events safely. She couldn't give that up.

"I'll sleep better tonight," she said. "Perhaps you can find something to help me with that."

"Sure. I have some ideas."

∞

Despite her promise that they'd go near Denise and the inn as little as possible during their off time, Joanna suggested the bar again. She wanted to check if the guest from 213 showed up without his wife. If he did...She wasn't sure what that meant.

To her surprise, she saw them sitting at a table. At least Joanna assumed the woman had to be the wife. She remembered the dress she was wearing as one of the ones she'd seen on the bed. Like Denise had said, she seemed a good deal younger than the man, but definitely not a minor. Reason to be relieved?

"Excuse me," she said to Rue who had followed her gaze. "I'll be right back."

Joanna got up and walked over to the couple's table. She could tell from the irritation in the man's gaze that he didn't recognize her right away.

"Good evening. I don't mean to disturb you, but I just wanted to check if the air conditioning is giving you any more trouble."

To her surprise, he gave her a polite smile.

"Oh, no, it's working perfectly, right, honey?"

The woman smiled, too, mumbling something unintelligible. She kept her head down.

"Thank you. If that's all? I'm afraid my wife isn't very comfortable around strangers."

"That's okay. You both have a good night."

Something wasn't right, and there was no way that Joanna could silence her own inner voice any longer.

"What are you going to do?" Rue asked, sounding resigned. She'd been able to tell from Joanna's body language that this story wasn't finished yet.

"I don't know yet, but I'll have to talk to Denise some more. If there's anything criminal going on, once they leave it will be too late."

"Are you sure you aren't about to get involved in something that's none of your business?"

"He could be abusing her."

"You don't think I'm scared of the same thing?" Rue's fork on the plate made a startling sound when she set it down. "I'm sorry, okay? I know that you could have decided to stay out of it, and then I wouldn't be here. We wouldn't be here. You'd probably still have a good job and be married."

Ironic to find that they obsessed about the same things.

"I have a good job, and I'm happy to be here with you. But you're right to say that those are different stories. Before...I knew what was going on. That's why I couldn't stay away. Right now, I don't know if I have a right to be worried, or if I'm just nosy. They could be the type of people to come to a place like this and have arguments the whole time. Vanessa and Theo aren't always on the same page."

"But you never assumed he could be abusing her." Rue cast a quick look at the other table where the man was still smiling. They could see the woman only from the back.

"I'm afraid I could miss my shot. I could run the risk of embarrassing myself—or her."

"It's better to be embarrassed than dead," Rue said dryly. "How are we going to do this?"

"I have to talk to Denise. We'll figure something out. You don't have to do anything."

"Oh, come on. You really think you can keep me out of this? Besides, I'm the one who's been training. I love that you've been brushing up on your piano lessons, but I don't think that's going to help us with this case."

Just like that, there was a case. Some things never changed, no matter how far you tried to run.

⁂

Despite her reassurances, it was clear that the situation put a lot of stress on Rue. At times she worked it off in ways that were more than pleasant for Joanna who had found a partner in her that completed her more than anyone could. After she'd worked for Joanna's father, the quiet polite assistant, people tended to underestimate Rue. Joanna knew better, had since the moment they met. Rue had told her she liked to take the lead, and she didn't exaggerate.

Joanna hadn't known that she'd be able to lose herself in a moment of perfect oblivion, until she could, trusting Rue with her body completely.

This dynamic was part of who they were. In the aftermath of Rue's abduction, it was also a way she was reclaiming her autonomy and safety, to feel at home in her body again.

Her ways of stress relief did wonders for Joanna. Tonight was no exception. She lay back, in awe, Rue snuggling into her arms, still half on top of her.

When she was sure her voice wouldn't fail her, Joanna asked, "You feel better now?" Her fingers lazily brushed over Rue's hair.

"It's a start," Rue murmured.

The joke Joanna might have made was lost in the exquisite shiver sneaking down her spine. They had overcome so many obstacles. This would be no exception.

"True. We can sleep in tomorrow…No appointments, except…"

"Except for a little detective work?"

"That's right. But that's tomorrow."

"Yes, it is."

She would sleep tonight.

Chapter Three

Denise had agreed to distract Mr. Farrell in 213 when she saw him alone. Rue, close by, called Joanna on her cell phone, and she hurried to get up to the room and knocked quickly.

There was no answer.

"Mrs. Farrell? Could I speak to you for a moment?" Joanna kept her voice down, not wanting to alert the other guests. She knocked again. If need be, she could come up with another cover story, but she didn't want to expose the woman. Farrell would be suspicious if he found her here.

A few more seconds ticked by. They felt like an eternity to Joanna. Finally, the door was opened a few inches.

"My husband isn't here."

"That's all right. I wanted to talk to you." This was the moment of truth. She'd either make a fool out of herself or change the trajectory of someone's life.

"Why?" She made no move to open the door further.

"Can I come in?"

While Mrs. Farrell was still pondering the question, another door opened at the end of the corridor and a woman walked out, from the looks of it ready to go to the beach. The inn employed a driver who brought tourists back and forth to the airport and the beach. When the woman saw Mrs. Farrell, her eyes widened.

She kept walking. Mrs. Farrell appeared spooked. She grabbed Joanna by the arm and pulled her inside with surprising force. Maybe Rue had a point when she said Joanna needed to work out more often.

"What do you want?"

"Check on you, make sure you're okay."

"Why wouldn't I be? I'm here with my husband." She had a faint Eastern European accent. Joanna didn't want to give in to preconceived notions, but she couldn't help wondering how the two had met.

"Is he treating you all right?"

Mrs. Farrell looked straight at her. Clearly, Joanna had offended her. She wasn't certain as to the reason. A quick visual check revealed no bruises, which didn't mean anything at all. On the job, she'd met abusers who made sure the obvious signs always stayed hidden under clothes, until the victim ended up in the ER.

"Go away."

"We can help you."

"I don't need your help."

She had heard that too. "If you ever change your mind, just give me or Denise a sign. You have other options."

"You don't know what you're talking about." Her tone was biting, her accent more pronounced. "I'd prefer if you leave us alone from now on."

"I'm sorry if I went too far. I hope you'll enjoy your vacation...and my offer still stands."

Joanna left the room, trying to fight her growing confusion. When she heard the elevator, she turned back and took the stairs down to the lobby. Denise was behind the counter.

"What happened?" she asked anxiously.

"Nothing much, to be honest. She denies she needs help. I told her she could always come to us if necessary."

"I'd really hate it if that kind of thing was going on under my roof," she said. "Well, of course I hate it in general, but...You know what I mean."

"I do."

"I'll have to give you an extra day of vacation after involving you in all of this."

"You don't have to. But we'd take it."

Later on, Joanna walked Rue to her training and went back to the house, going over the conversation with Mrs. Farrell in her mind. She powered up her laptop and did a quick search, finding many Farrells, but not the couple that occupied #213. She remembered the look the woman from 217 had given Mrs. Farrell. Had she imagined that? Joanna shook her head. She wasn't making things up. Mrs. Farrell had been quick to let her in after she'd seen the other woman. Was the husband straying? Was that why the couple had arguments?

In that case, it was truly none of her business. Her own parents had had many of those arguments before her mother packed her bags one day when Joanna was in school. When she came home, only the housekeeper was waiting for her, telling her the news with a sympathetic gaze. She had also notified Lawrence Mitchell. He came back after dinner that night, curt and unwilling to answer the many questions Joanna had. He didn't seem much distraught about the departure of his wife.

Nothing much could rattle Lawrence, because there was very little he cared about. The business, and his party friends, always came first.

Joanna sat down at the piano again, brushing her fingers over the keys. In retrospect, it surprised her that he didn't consider her taking lessons, and showing only moderate talent, a waste of time. Then again, she didn't get to know him all that well. She started playing a melody from memory. Still rusty, still stumbling. She tried again.

Lost in the play, she didn't even realize how much time had passed until she realized she wasn't alone any longer. Rue had tears in her eyes.

"What happened?" Joanna asked, alarmed, on her feet a second later.

"Wow. I had no idea you were this good."

"Come on. I'm not."

"It is beautiful."

Bittersweet, maybe, drawing her into memories she tried to push aside for the most part. Regrets that were pointless to ponder in the present.

"My dad never tried to contact my mother. He just let her go. He let her go long before she left."

"Perhaps that was what she wanted—or needed." Rue reached out to brush her fingers against Joanna's cheek. "We don't know."

"No, we don't. But I don't want you to ever doubt that you're more important to me than anything or anyone else. I still can't say for sure what their deal is, but I wanted the woman to know she has someone to go to if she needs to."

"I understand that. I love you." Rue held on tight, halting her pointless trip down memory lane. If it wasn't for the course of events that had brought them here, Joanna might have tried to find her mother someday, look for answers.

As it was, she was unlikely to see either of her parents again, but that was a choice they had made for her. No use going back.

"I love you too. You still want to go to the museum today?"

They had said no plans but sitting around for too long made them both antsy.

"Yes, I'd love to."

For the next two hours, they browsed the exhibitions at the local art museum, something they hadn't gotten around to do earlier. They finished the tour with a cappuccino at the small café.

Mr. and Mrs. Ferrell sat at a table near the entrance. As usual, he was doing the talking, while she listened, looking morose. Preconceived notions, or justified instinct, this type of relationship made her skin crawl, and she sensed that Rue felt the same.

"Let's take that coffee to go," she said. From here, it wasn't far to the beach, and they enjoyed their beverage listening to the waves.

They returned home soon after. Much as she tried to relax, she couldn't get rid of that antsy, restless feeling. After they had dinner and cleaned the dishes, Joanna gave up the pretense.

"There's something I need to talk to Denise about," she said to Rue who looked up from the book she was reading. She didn't seem to suspect anything.

"It can't wait?"

"It will take just a few minutes," Joanna assured her. "I'll be right back."

The woman in 217 didn't look surprised to see her.

"I was wondering when you'd come," she said. Joanna detected the same faint accent she had heard in Mrs. Farrell's voice.

"Why did you think I'd come?"

"You think something bad is going on behind that other door? I think you're right. Come on in."

Joanna saw that she'd made a rum and coke from the small bottles in the mini bar.

"You'd like one?"

"No, thanks."

"I tried to talk to her, but she won't let me."

"Do you think Mrs. Farrell is in immediate danger?"

The answer wasn't as conclusive as Joanna had hoped.

"She might be. She sure as hell isn't safe."

"How do you know that?"

"I'm Tamara," the woman said. "She's Alexandra. We paid the same lousy people for a promise."

It didn't take Joanna long to make possible connections, reminding her that expecting the worst of people wasn't always exaggerated.

"Let me guess, when you arrived here, you didn't get the jobs you were promised."

Tamara nodded before she took a sip of her drink. "You sure you don't want anything? I don't tell the story that often, but if I had to listen to it, I'd want to drink too."

"I was a cop once," Joanna said. "I understand wanting to drink."

"I'm sure you do. Anyway, I don't know what happened to Alex, but I heard she tried to get away, and they roughed her up badly. I don't know if I'm paranoid, or if this is a coincidence, her being here with that man."

"Do you know him?"

Tamara shook her head. "I've never met him in person, but he must be one of the final clients. That's what they called it sometimes. A permanent placement."

"So, what you're saying is, he..." Joanna's stomach churned at the thought. "Bought her?" Of course, she knew better than most that monsters blended in, some of them soft-spoken polite men in suits. Decker had been the quiet friendly neighbor next door. Edward Short regularly visited his mother. Both of them had displayed a rabid hate for women in their crimes.

"If you want to call it that. Money sure exchanged hands. Lots of it."

Joanna didn't want to hear any more, but she knew she couldn't stop. Denise would have to contact the authorities. She only had a brief thought about what that would mean for her and Rue.

"What about you?"

"There were people that helped me get out, people who hate these men just as much. This is why I'm here in the first place. Before that...I guess I was lucky, in comparison. They put me with a family who needed a nanny. They hid my passport and only withheld food when they thought I needed to be taught a lesson."

"My God." Joanna was curious as to the mysterious saviors, but most of all she could feel a familiar emotion taking over: Red hot anger. She shook herself. This wasn't about her, or the victims she'd tried to get justice for.

"I think God had little to do with it, but I see the irony in them coming here for whatever it is. Someone might be watching them. Or me." She finished her glass in one gulp. "Few of us escape, but when that happens, they try to bring us back. Not because of the money they lost, but mostly to teach us a lesson." Tamara was right. Joanna did want to drink, to erase what she'd heard, to erase what she already knew.

"The people who helped you, do you have a way to contact them?"

"No. That was part of the deal, supposedly safer for them and me. It was very quick, middle of the night. They made sure I had papers and a place to stay."

That sounded a lot like the work of Vanessa's friend who had gotten Joanna, and later, Rue to the island. By-the-book Joanna had been naïve in ways she now had a hard time believing...until the day she realized the full weight of the law would never been enough, for her, or the families and friends of Decker's victims. The day she decided she was going to act on her own rules.

Joanna wasn't the only one, and she wistfully admitted that the work of those other people was a lot more helpful in the long term.

"Okay. I'll talk to my boss, and we'll get Alexandra some help. The police might have some questions for you."

Tamara sat up straighter.

"I don't know if I can do it. What if they want to know about the people who helped me?"

"I'm sure they'll be more concerned about a case of human trafficking. If they ask, you tell them the same thing you told me. They got you out of a desperate situation. You don't know how to find them. We need to act before they leave."

"I'm aware. Could you just let me talk to her first?"

"You said she won't let you."

"I'll try harder. Please."

"It's too dangerous. He's with her now. The police will know what steps to take." Joanna wasn't sure about the size of the police force on the island, but given the magnitude of the alleged crime, they'd sure call in the FBI. They'd start by questioning the Farrells. Joanna hoped that would give Alexandra time enough to get away from him.

"They might deport her. Or me. I don't want to ever go back. I'd rather go back to that family."

"Okay, give me until tomorrow. We'll figure something out. I swear." Joanna was afraid she was going to lose her if she insisted, even though she was fairly certain there was no way around contacting the police. "I appreciate you talking to me. I know it can't be easy."

Tamara studied her with curiosity. "How come you aren't a cop any longer?"

After a moment of hesitation, Joanna chose the truth.

"I killed two men who had murdered women." When Tamara waited in silence, her expression impassive, she elaborated,

"It wasn't self-defense. Or at least, some people didn't see it as such."

"I trust you. I'll talk to Alex again."

"Thank you."

Tamara followed her to the door, and Joanna waited, sensing that she had more to say.

"Like I said, things weren't so bad for me once they sold me off. Before that...let's say, at times, dreaming of killing them was the thing that kept me sane."

"I know," Joanna said.

"Yes. I'll talk to you tomorrow."

Chapter Four

When she knocked on the door to Denise's office and entered after Denise told her to, Joanna was barely surprised to see Rue sitting in one of the chairs.

"This is going to be a long night, I'm afraid," Denise said. "Joanna?"

"These two women were trafficked, one into domestic labor, the alleged Mrs. Farrell likely sold into sexual slavery."

Both Denise and Rue flinched.

"Tamara doesn't want to talk to the police, but I think we need to call them, get the ball rolling. This is bigger than the island."

"You know that this will mean exposure for you as well...possibly Rue?"

Joanna caught Rue's gaze on her. She didn't seem mad or afraid, just tired.

"I can't speak for Rue, but for me, I'm willing to risk it. This woman needs help now."

In addition to Alexandra's urgent situation, Tamara had raised the idea that the two of them meeting in this place might not be a coincidence. The men that trafficked her could be trying to get her back, to "teach her a lesson" as she'd called it.

They needed the help of law enforcement. Joanna looked at Rue again. "Nothing will happen to you, I swear."

But how would the authorities, the ones back in the city, deal with her abrupt departure if they found out where she was? Would they still go after Vanessa—or Theo? But Theo had never known the whole truth, and if anyone wanted to go after Vanessa, they would have by now. Someone with a high-profile career like hers, they would have found something on the Internet.

"It's okay. I'm in," Rue said.

"All right." Denise took a deep breath. "Let's do this."

Most of the guests were inside when the police arrived to take Mr. Farrell in for questioning. Some were watching from their windows. None of them were allowed to go near the operation, but when the cops led Farrell away in handcuffs, he spotted Joanna.

"You are making a big mistake," he sneered.

Not as big as the one you made, she thought, but didn't say it out loud. She saw another policeman talking to Alexandra who was shaking her head and crying. Joanna could only imagine what Farrell might have told her, or what he had over her. She turned away in disgust for people like him.

No longer her business. Maybe now was the time to rest.

"Miss?" one of the policemen called to her. Not yet. Sighing to no one, she went to join him.

Tamara and Alexandra sat at a table in the breakfast room the next morning. Tamara seemed excited, while Alexandra was wearing the same unhappy expression as before. It was probably hard for her to believe that the nightmare could come to an end.

"You did everything you could," Rue told her. "It's still, you know, vacation? You remember?"

"Of course I do. Denise even said something about an extra day though I'm not sure she was serious about it."

"I love you," Rue said with surprising passion. "And sometimes you frustrate the hell out of me."

"Oh. I sense a backhanded compliment."

"Maybe that's something I need to discuss with Dr. Shepherd. Me, being selfish. Sometimes I just want you all to myself, but you can't do that, can you? You have to take on everybody's pain, even here and now. But what do I know? You had a suspicion, and you were right." She shook her head. "I annoy myself. It's not that I'm not glad for her."

"I know that you are. The timing wasn't the best."

"No, it wasn't, but then again, the timing will never be great. We can never pretend these things don't exist. At some point in my life...I could. Sometimes I want to go back to being that naïve and ignorant."

"I understand. I've felt this way."

Rue waited until the waitress had filled their cups with coffee. She drank from hers and sighed.

"Not a conversation I should start, ever, before caffeine. I just get so afraid I could lose you all over again."

Joanna knew about being afraid. The time from when she knew for sure that the slasher had taken Rue, to the moment she was safe, had been the worst in her life. She reasoned it might not be a good idea to share these thoughts.

"I'll do better. We go back to what we know, you discuss these things with Dr. Shepherd, and kick ass in the ring. I'll...get back to my mediocre piano skills. None of it will happen before caffeine."

Despite herself, Rue had to laugh. "How do you put up with this? Me?"

"You're really good in bed," Joanna said matter-of-factly, almost making her choke on her coffee. She saw that Tamara and Alexandra had left the table. If there was anything to follow up on, Denise would let them know, otherwise the case was blessedly out of their hands.

⁂

She had not meant to reduce their relationship to one single aspect, but when they returned home, it turned out that the mood was just right. Joanna fell asleep with the soft sound of the fan's blades whirring overhead. Selfish, who could say? She loved being the sole center of Rue's attention and giving her the same focus in return. They had done their share once again. She wanted them to spend the following days indulging themselves, sleep, sex, food, and drinks. Wasn't that the logical thing to do in paradise?

The monsters might return from time to time, but they wouldn't win.

Chapter Five

Joanna was sleeping so peacefully, Rue didn't want to wake her up just to tell her she was about to go out of her skin. She couldn't understand how Joanna could go from being all involved in the mystery of room 213 back to vacation. Maybe that was a skill she had learned during her time as a cop.

It was a skill that eluded Rue, no matter how hard she tried. She had needed all the time from the incident to the present moment to even think about slowing down and enjoying a vacation, like normal people did.

Everything she'd told Joanna about feeling selfish, and feeling bad about it, had been the truth. She was aware, but she couldn't stop it either. Next time, Dr. Shepherd likely wouldn't end the session ten minutes early. Rue had a lot to learn. She sighed, carefully slipped out of bed, and went into the small office where she powered up the computer. They were safe here, or so Joanna kept insisting. The people who had made their new life possible, knew what they were doing, had provided the same service for other women in need.

Only that wasn't exactly what Rue and Joanna were, was it? It didn't matter now. They used the Internet sparsely, because search histories and other online activities could be traced...If someone bothered tracing them.

But now Joanna had spoken to the police, and that changed everything. They didn't need fingerprints or DNA—a few keystrokes, and they'd easily find her story.

Rue identified the emotion that was making her light-headed and restless, as anger. Truth be told, she'd felt it more or less since Vanessa had told her what she'd done. Rue had never been sure if she'd made Joanna's situation better or worse, but coming here to this peaceful place placated her. Now, it was Joanna who had potentially made a decision that affected the two of them.

To help a woman in need.

Rue clicked the button and waited for the ring tone. After a couple of times, she saw the smiling face of her mother on the screen.

"Rue, hi! How are you?"

Bought and sold. How bad a person was she to envy Alexandra for Joanna's attention and concern?

"We're fine. On vacation actually."

"That's why you're in your PJs at noon?"

Rue blushed at the implications, all of which were true.

"We slept in," she said, blushing even more. "I just wanted to check in, see how you all are."

"Good. The weather's nice, probably not as nice as where you are, but we have the barbecue out."

All of their conversations were fairly superficial, but neither Rue nor her parents cared. They were part of a small niche she had carved out for herself, and she wasn't going to give it up. It was part of Rue's new normalcy.

"That sounds great."

"We had some friends over too. Oh, that's the doorbell. I'm sorry I have to go, this might be Dad's birthday present. Say hello to Joanna for us."

"I'm here. Hi, Mrs. Carmichael."

"Joanna, it's great to see you! I'm afraid I've got to go! I'll see you next time?"

"Probably," Joanna said after the screen had already gone dark. She still stood in the same space, leaning against the doorway.

Rue wanted to give her a reasonable explanation, but she couldn't find anything that wouldn't sound angry or defensive.

"How long have you been doing this?" Joanna's tone was neutral, if anything, tinged with surprise. Because she hadn't found out earlier, or because Rue had kept something from her? Another scene sprang to mind, and all of a sudden, she wanted to cry. Why hadn't she seen the similarities before? Would Joanna? Why *wouldn't* she?

"Since my first week here. After everything that happened, I couldn't let them think I just vanished."

"I thought Vanessa had taken care of that."

"Yes, but I wasn't sure they'd believe her. I found it hard to believe when she kept insisting that you were okay."

That brought something akin to a smile to Joanna's face. Rue realized that she'd suggested Vanessa wasn't trustworthy enough.

"I had to do it. Not very often, and not for long, just to make sure everything's all right."

"Okay. We can't turn back the time on that, but you know these things can be traced, right?"

"And why would I care?" Joanna flinched at Rue raising her voice. She had startled herself. There was no turning back now. "Sure, I did that only for me, so it's not the same as you talking to the police. You don't think they ran your name and have realized by now that somewhere far away, the authorities would like to talk to you? How long do you think it will take them to come here for more questions? And you honestly worry about me talking to my parents?"

"I'm sorry you feel that way, but it's not the same. Here on the island, we can keep it contained. Denise knows someone...They're not going to tell on us. All they wanted was my statement regarding Mrs. Farrell."

"You think that's it? I can't believe how naïve you are sometimes!"

In an instant, the room had become claustrophobic to Rue, something she'd experienced often after her abduction, but never before on the island, not even after the night terrors. She couldn't stand herself, but Joanna was the only one she could run away from, temporarily, to make a dubious point.

"Rue, wait! Let's talk about this!"

She couldn't imagine words that would help at this moment. Rue fled from the house and all but ran all the way to the inn, and the gym. Zach was in the ring with another student, but she changed into workout clothes anyway. He'd make time for her.

❦

Rue had cried in the shower, and she wasn't sure she was done yet, but at least the fog in her head was starting to clear. That didn't make her feel much better, just embarrassed, for the way she had reacted.

"You want to tell me what the emergency was?" Zach asked when she returned from the locker room.

She shook her head.

"Not really."

They had talked, in the beginning, about her choices and goals...

"I want to make sure that what happened to me will never happen again," she had told him that day, aware that her statement was open to many interpretations.

"This doesn't come with a guarantee."

38

"A change of odds is enough."

Was it? Rue had suppressed parts of the traumatic experience, but she remembered the man, Edward Short, a serial killer wanted for more than a decade, pushing her down on the frozen ground. Thinking of a self-defense class she'd taken, none of the lessons coming back to her. This time had to be different.

"He didn't rape me, though I'm not sure that was never on the table. This...was more his thing."

Zach's eyes widened slightly when she lifted her shirt and showed him the faint, but visible scars on her stomach.

"Ex-boyfriend?"

"Notorious serial killer."

"When can you start?"

Forcing herself back to the present, Rue continued, "Bad day. I needed to get this out of my system."

"I heard the police arrested one of the guests. That must have brought up some stuff. I'm sorry."

"Yeah, me too. Thanks for making time. See you."

He touched her shoulder briefly, a familiar, friendly touch. Rue straightened and turned to leave, hoping Joanna would be waiting for her outside the gym.

She wasn't.

⁂

Much to her credit, Dr. Shepherd had warned her about the bad days. Rue had brushed her off, because wasn't she an expert already? How much worse could it get than waking up screaming, in a cold sweat? First the hospital, then her own apartment. She couldn't stand to have people around her, even her parents and Vanessa, and she couldn't stand to be alone.

For a while, she had managed to dull down her overactive senses, some of it prescribed medication, some of it, self-medicating…until Vanessa made her the offer she couldn't refuse, and wasn't it a good thing she hadn't?

A bad day on the island wasn't the same, because they were surrounded by beauty Rue had only seen on TV and the Internet before. Because Joanna loved her, enough to give up a life with her when she thought it was what she needed to do, enough to welcome her here when it became an option. Nature was healing her. Being with Joanna was healing her, but what if it all came to an end today?

Joanna had broken up with her before, that one time, because Rue had kept secrets.

Where would she go if she couldn't stay?

She had to find Joanna. She had to find the right words.

Joanna wasn't home. Rue went back to the inn, wandering around its grounds looking for Joanna without any success. Was she still angry? Did she have reason to be? Vanessa had asked Rue how attached she was to her life in the city, before making the offer. It wasn't Rue's fault that Joanna wasn't in touch with her parents, or that they didn't care.

Denise's office was closed, so Rue went back to the lobby, and for some reason that eluded her, she stepped into the elevator, taking it up to the second floor.

The two men with the large suitcases made her feel crowded, even though they barely seemed to notice her. Perhaps she'd find Joanna with Tamara, checking up on her, because…Her day had to be as bad as Rue's, if not worse.

Rue went to knock on #217, encountering another closed door.

When she walked back to the elevator, she realized that the door to 213 wasn't closed.

Leave it alone.

It was her first impulse ever since she'd made it out of that horrible place, ever since she knew that she'd live. Curiosity had killed more than the cat. Alexandra had probably left already, and a maid was cleaning the room. None of her business.

Rue knocked on the door.

"Hello? Alexandra? Are you in here?"

No answer. She gently pushed the door open and went inside the room, freezing at the sight. Her own scream jolted her out of her paralysis, then Rue reached for her cell phone with trembling hands and called for an ambulance.

Chapter Six

A chunk of time was missing from her memory, once again. Rue recognized the signs, the fog in her mind, the persisting nausea. She had thrown up already and was currently trying to make her stomach cooperate as she lay on the sofa Denise kept in her office.

Joanna sat next to her, her hand softly brushing over Rue's forehead.

"This feels good, but don't stay to close. I don't want to throw up on you."

"You're going to be okay."

Between the touch and the warm tone, Rue could almost pretend that their earlier argument had never happened. Regardless, she needed to know.

"You're still mad at me?" she asked.

"I'm not mad," Joanna assured her. "We need to talk about these things...but not now."

"You're not going to kick me out?"

"What? No. Are you sure you didn't pass out and hit your head?"

Rue started laughing until she realized Joanna's question was serious.

"No. No, I didn't. Farrell, is he...?"

"Dead, yes. I suppose someone didn't want him to talk." Joanna shook her head. "What was he doing there anyway? He wasn't supposed to get out yet."

Rue had no answer for her, so she blurted out the first thing that was on her mind.

"My head hurts."

"I can imagine. You were pretty sick. I'm so sorry. I imagine the police will want to talk to us—again—and we can take it easy for the rest of the day."

Whatever that meant.

"I'm sorry. It's all my fault. I should have never gone in there."

Upon a closer look, she realized Joanna looked pale and worried.

"None of this is your fault. Now that that's out of the way, did you see anyone? In the elevator?"

Some of the events from the cabin had never broken through the fog. Despite her headache, Rue realized that Joanna's calm questions were triggering fractions of memories. She'd been lost in thought, for some reason almost ducking into the wall...

Rue bolted upright on the couch, feeling like she was on a shaking boat, about to be seasick. She managed to hold back the impulse.

"Not in the elevator. They were in the hallway. Oh my God. It must have been them!"

Before Rue could ask about Alexandra and Tamara, Denise entered the room with two cops, a man and a woman.

"These detectives need to talk to you," she said tersely.

Rue wanted to disappear. Everything she had accused Joanna of, she had brought upon them as well. She assumed that her video chats with her parents still were the least of their problems.

❧

"Thank you for your time. We'll be in touch."

Even Rue recognized the standard phrase that meant they weren't entirely off the hook.

She hadn't mentioned the argument, of course, but described how she'd passed by the two men, and a moment later, found Farrell's body.

"I thought Joanna might want to check up on Tamara." She cast Joanna, who hadn't left the room, an apologetic look. The cops didn't seem to mind her presence. It was the only reason Rue was still hanging on. "When nobody was there, I wanted to go back, and I noticed that the door of 213 was open. With everything that happened before...It was stupid to go in, I know."

"You couldn't know if there was still danger," the female detective acknowledged. "Can you describe the men?"

"White. Burly. Late forties, I don't know. They didn't say anything."

"And you said they both had big suitcases?"

"Yes. Have you talked to Tamara? Or Mrs. Farell? Was she ever even married to him?" Rue noticed that her words had come out in rapid succession, and she forced herself to take a breath.

The cops exchanged a meaningful look. Rue didn't know what to make of Joanna's expression.

"They are both missing," the male detective said. "At this moment, we assume that the men who killed Mr. Farrell, have taken them."

"Rue saw them. She described them to you. What are your plans for her protection?"

"I don't need any of that. They could have killed me in the hallway if they wanted to." Rue could barely believe the words that were coming out of her mouth. The day had gone from bad to so much worse within hours, she found it hard to contain the whiplash—or hold anything back.

"No, you're right," the male detective said to Joanna. "We'll assign an officer."

"When?"

"They're waiting outside. When we're done here, they'll go with you."

Joanna nodded, obviously satisfied with the answer. Rue wasn't sure she was.

"And then what, they just hang out everywhere we go? The island isn't that big. I'm sure that whoever killed Farrell, is on a plane or a boat already, trying to get out. Isn't that where you should concentrate your efforts?"

She half expected them to laugh at her, but no one did.

"We have called in help from the mainland. Your safety is our priority."

"What about Alexandra and Tamara?"

"We'll find them," the woman said with a grim determination that felt comfortingly familiar to Rue.

If Joanna was okay with this, she had to be, too.

Rue wished they could do more for them. Without words, she knew that she and Joanna were on the same page.

<hr />

The officer, a man in his late twenties, followed them in the car when they went grocery shopping. This was as much an attempt at going back to some sort of normal, as it was a necessity, Rue had realized when she'd looked into the fridge.

They'd cook and eat at home tonight, perhaps offer the young man some of that grilled chicken with pineapple and mango.

"There was a moment when I thought I could never eat again," she confessed.

"It's been a pretty rough day." This had to be the understatement of the year. "We still need meals. The police will handle it from here. They seemed competent, don't you think?"

"Did they ever tell you how Farrell got out?"

Joanna's gaze hardened. "He got a lawyer pretty quickly, and they couldn't prove he knew that Alexandra was a trafficked woman. Until they find them...We'll it's too late for him now."

Delusion, death. It seemed like they could never get away from it for long. Rue's stomach lurched and settled again.

"I try not to think about it. But..."

"Yeah," Joanna said simply when seconds ticked by, and Rue didn't finish the sentence. They had to wait when a flock of sheep was crossing the street, and Joanna took her hand. "I hope the police find them soon, but this is not about us. We're safe."

To her utter amazement, Rue believed it, and it had little to do with the twenty-something year old officer in the car behind them.

❦

Officer Thompson accepted the meal with genuine thanks but declined the glass of wine Rue offered out of politeness. He checked in with his colleagues at regular intervals. No news so far.

Rue went back to the table she and Joanna occupied in the corner of the terrace and poured some wine for both of them.

"Like you said, it's been a rough day. Let's say everything we need to say, and move on? I'm sorry I kept a secret from you, and I broke a promise. I hope you believe me. It will never happen again."

"I know."

Her emotions were still close to the surface. If it wasn't for the officer sitting a few feet away, Rue's reaction to Joanna's quiet reassurance might have been a different one.

"We've been kidding ourselves, haven't we? To think there might be a safe place, anywhere in the world? The moment you care about someone, safety is out the window. It's an illusion." It might be the wine talking. It might be the cold hard truth. The fact that Joanna needed more than a few seconds to answer led her to believe it was the latter. What were they, then, jaded, or naïve?

"We are still safe. It will all go away."

"Did Decker go away? Or Short? I don't know. I'm sure though that Tamara felt safe, until the moment she saw Alexandra with that man."

"I'm sorry, I don't know the answer. There's no one hundred percent guarantee."

"Oh damn. Now you sound like Zach."

Joanna laughed softly. "That's not a bad thing? He's okay."

"Maybe I don't like to be reminded of my limitations," Rue said, though she had to smile too. "How messed up would it be if I wanted to go back to the museum tomorrow? Is it horrible to want to have a reasonably good day while other people are in danger?"

"It serves no one if you let it overwhelm you." Joanna cast a look at the policeman who had gotten up to check the perimeter. "Prison was like that sometimes," she continued. "I felt like I was wasting my time being inside when I could have been arresting criminals. Part of it was...Guilt, I guess. The other part, ego, to think there wouldn't be anyone doing the job just as well. We have told the truth, we have given them everything we could. I'm sorry if your question got lost in there somewhere, but no, it's not horrible to want to go to the museum. It's a privilege, but not horrible."

"Maybe he'll enjoy the art too."

"Maybe."

❧

Strange how the same painting, the same sculpture, could hold an entirely different meaning on a different day. The last time they'd walked around these rooms, Rue had felt happy and light. Now she saw some of her own pain echoed in the artists' voices, in details she hadn't noticed before.

Joanna was right. What happened didn't negate the progress they'd made before. For sure, the local police had a lot on their plate right now. Her new life with Joanna was still priority.

They stopped at the café once again, and this time sat down with their coffee, Officer Thompson at a table close by.

No one had tried to bother or follow them. What she'd blurted out in a moment of bravado or frustration probably held true: The men were gone. That part was a relief. The part where Alexandra and Tamara might be with them, not so much. Except if...

"Remember when Tamara told you to hold off on talking to the police?"

"Yes," Joanna said. "She thought they might deport them."

"What if that's the reason they're gone? Maybe no one took them, but they ran away together?" Rue was warming up to the theory, getting excited over it in a way that might be premature.

Joanna sat up straighter. "You think they might have to do something with Farrell's death?"

"They wouldn't be the first women forced to take matters into their own hands, would they?" Think, before you talk. "No, that's not what I meant. Perhaps there's no relation. They took off. Farrell's contacts wanted to take care of loose ends."

Joanna's gaze was apologetic, almost sympathetic, and it wasn't until then that Rue noticed the holes in her brilliant theory. If it happened to be true, the two women might have the police and a couple of murderers after them.

"Oh God, that was really naïve of me to think there could be any good to this, wasn't it?"

"Not naïve. Perhaps a bit too hopeful."

Rue made a non-committal sound. "That's a kind way to put it. Thank you for indulging me today...and every day."

"Told you why. Seriously. You came to be with me. This is more than anyone could ask...I've thought about this a long time. I think—"

The waitress brought the cake and coffee they had ordered.

"What do you think?" Rue asked, feeling that an important moment just had been interrupted.

"I'm incredibly grateful for you," Joanna said. "That's all."

☙

The day passed without incident. Before they were about to go home, late in the afternoon, Thompson got a call.

"Good news," he said when he got back to them. "One of the men has been caught on the mainland. They think it's safe for you now."

"What about the other?" Joanna asked the obvious question before Rue could.

"The search is still on, but they assume he's laying low. I'm sure they'll find him."

"Well, thanks, anyway."

"That was a bit anticlimactic," Rue said when they were in the car.

"Fine with me. They are making progress. That's a good sign."

Rue wondered if Tamara and Alexandra appreciated progress, wherever they were, and decided it wasn't a fair response. Life hadn't been fair to them, or her, or Joanna. Considering, she and Joanna had done pretty well with the deck they'd been dealt.

"It is. I hope they find them soon. I'll call Dr. Shepherd tomorrow. I think I need to see her."

"That's a good idea." When Rue shrugged, Joanna elaborated, "You're taking care of yourself. It's not easy. Believe me, I know."

"You'd like to come?"

"No. But I'll wait for you downstairs."

Rue decided this was a subject for another day. "Okay."

Back home, they went out onto the deck. Rue had picked up a paperback, and Joanna went inside to mix cocktails for the two of them.

Before, mysteries had been her choice more often than not, but in recent times, Rue had found solace in romance. Perhaps it was that she so desperately needed to believe in happy endings.

She was on her feet an instant later when she heard the breaking glass.

Chapter Seven

"**D**on't shoot!" Alexandra pleaded. Joanna sighed in relief as she lowered the gun. She had arranged for it early on during her stay on the island, but only recently started to carry again. She had hoped she'd never have to use it. Most of the time they'd been living here, she'd even forgotten about it.

Rue was in the kitchen a second later, brandishing a vase she set down with a curse when she realized who their visitor was.

"I'm really sorry," Alexandra said. "It turns out I do need your help."

"All right. Let me clean this up and we can sit down and talk. I assume there's a reason you're hiding from the police."

"I don't know if I can trust them. I trust you."

Tamara had said the same thing. Joanna wondered if they didn't put far too much faith in her. Didn't they realize how limited her options were? She was glad Alexandra seemed unharmed. But what could they do for her?

She cleared the glass she had dropped earlier off the floor while Rue went to put the vase back. Then she poured a drink for each of them. Alexandra accepted hers gratefully. On second thought, Joanna took a bag of chips out of the pantry and added some cheese on a plate.

"Do you know what happened? In the hotel? And with Tamara?"

Alexandra put her glass down on the table as if she no longer had the appetite. "I don't know. They shot Harry. I ran...I don't think they saw me, but I'm sure they know who I am. I think they took Tamara."

"They came for her? You know anything about that?"

Alexandra shook her head with a bitter smile. "It's not like they tell me things. I'm not even sure Harry knew. The only thing I know is that you can never get out. They tell you that if you try, they'll find you anywhere, and it seems to be true, no?"

"They haven't found you," Joanna said, searching Rue's gaze. A lifetime of apologies wouldn't be enough for drawing her into this or allowing her to be drawn into it—Joanna wasn't even sure what was more patronizing or wrong. It had all started as a simple act of kindness. They were in over their heads, all of them—Joanna, Rue, Denise and the two women, the fate of one still unclear. "For what it's worth, they arrested one of the killers. It would make a lot of sense for the other guy to lay low."

"Or to come back for the last witness."

Rue flinched.

"Honestly, I don't think that's what they're going to do. The police are looking for him, and for Tamara."

"I don't know if that's a good thing."

"What do you think we can do for you?"

"Tamara told me you killed someone. Bad men. In my experience, when they come for you, it's best not to hesitate. Most of the cops might be okay, but what if they promised something to only one of them? Blackmailed them? I can't take the risk."

It had been Joanna's cue to flinch. Everything Alexandra said was true, but she had hoped to come to a point in her life when she wasn't reminded daily of those facts.

"When did you last talk to Tamara?"

"The other night." Alexandra shook her head, tears glistening in her eyes. "How naïve we were thinking this was all over. It never is."

Joanna didn't realize she was pacing until she came to a halt in the middle of room. This was all wrong. Alexandra and Tamara needed a lot more help than she and Rue could give them. If she'd still been with the department, she'd have options, connect them with services for women who had been abused. She didn't want to give Alexandra false hope, but she couldn't deny the possibilities either. It only took one cop willing to look the other way. It wasn't unheard of.

Joanna wasn't worried about herself, but she couldn't put Rue at risk.

"This is what we'll do. You can stay the night, and how about in the morning I check in with the officer, see if there's any news on Tamara and the second man? It's a small community. They wouldn't be so surprised that we want to follow up."

"I'm sorry I didn't tell you the truth at first," Alexandra said. "Perhaps, for a while, I didn't even know what the truth was anymore. Seeing Tamara...It shook me."

"I can imagine." Joanna had many more questions, none of which she wanted to ask in Rue's presence.

"I despised him at times, but he wasn't the one I wanted dead. He was naïve, and they used him too."

"He committed a crime. Not one that warrants death, as you said, but he should have gone away for a long time. He shouldn't even have been in that room." The words were out before Joanna could remember that perhaps telling herself this story about Farrell had helped Alexandra survive—and when it came to the right kind of justice, or what it meant, her record was sketchy at best. "Were you actually married?" she asked.

"Oh yes. Appearances mattered to him."

Joanna had the flash of a memory, Decker's widow sitting in the courtroom with her baby, her face tear streaked. Farrell might not have been a sadistic killer, but in her opinion, he didn't deserve much sympathy either. If he'd been looking for a date, an equal partner instead of a prisoner, he would likely still be alive. But Farrell wasn't the most pressing problem.

Worst case scenario, there was a mole in the police, and they had no interest in helping Tamara. Someone might want to tie up loose ends, and Alexandra wasn't the only one.

Rue could describe the men.

The premise had changed quickly, and not in their favor. Now Alexandra was here, another reason for Farrell's contacts not to leave town yet.

"Alexandra, would you mind if I talked to Rue alone for a moment? We'll be just outside."

"I came to your house asking for help. Of course I don't mind."

When they were alone on the terrace, Rue spoke first.

"I don't know how she can hold it together." Even though the evening sun was warm, a violent shudder ran through her body. "It was only a few hours. For her...We don't even know."

"People do what they do to survive," Joanna offered. This might be the best possible way to start the conversation. "For the moment, we're all safe."

"But that might change soon," Rue finished her thought, looking resigned.

"I don't know that it will, but I'm not going to take any chances. Rue..."

She didn't need to say it out loud. Rue's eyes widened, and the color drained from her face.

"No."

"Hear me out, please."

"This was supposed to be the solution, right? The only way. The once in a lifetime chance. I agree that she needs help, but we're not going to throw this away. I won't."

"The police might want to question you, at worst. You just tell them you took a sabbatical. Your parents can confirm that you kept in touch. That's all. Nobody reported you missing."

"No, Joanna. There are too many variables in this. They might still find a way to trace it all back to you, and then it was all for nothing. Everything Vanessa did. The life we built here. You can't tell me you're ready to give up on all of this...on us."

Joanna reached out to embrace her, but Rue stepped back angrily.

"This is for us. We know the danger is real, and I don't think either of us can go through this again."

"And you'll do what? Be a sitting duck here with Alexandra? Or a martyr?"

The accusation struck, and it was as unwelcome as Alexandra's misplaced praise.

"I don't know!" She reminded herself that their guest didn't need to hear or care about their argument. "There you go. I'll admit it. I don't know what to do."

"We still have to make dinner."

Not waiting for an answer, Rue turned to go back inside.

***

Joanna hadn't told the whole truth. She had a pretty clear idea of what to do, even though she wasn't sure how to execute that plan. She couldn't bear to think about it too much either, because the outcome was beyond uncertain.

She called Denise and asked her about her conversations with the police, and everything regarding Tamara.

"I don't know more than you do," Denise said, surprised. "I understand this is all worrisome, but you should really try to find some distance. Remember your vacation will be over soon."

"Yeah, you keep telling me that. What about that guest who saw Tamara?"

"She said she saw Tamara when she went for a swim. That was the last time anyone saw her. I'm sorry, but there's nothing else. Let the police handle it?"

Where did I hear that before?

To Joanna's surprise, Denise followed up with an impassioned plea. "Please, Joanna, don't jinx it, okay? I know that if you had to go back, it would be difficult for both of you to say the least. We did everything we could to make life comfortable for you two."

Why did everyone seem to suggest she was exaggerating?

"I don't think Tamara's life is very comfortable right now."

"People are on it. I don't know what to tell you."

"I didn't ask you to tell me anything. Thanks anyway."

Neither Joanna and Rue nor their guest had the desire to raise any more uncomfortable subjects. They spent most of the evening in tense silence.

Joanna knew she couldn't do this without help. It was risky to contact the only people who might be able to assist in her efforts, but perhaps with Rue regularly talking to her parents, that ship had long sailed.

They had found peace with each other.

Everyone was right to tell her she was mad to jeopardize any of it.

Perhaps that's what Joanna was, mad, if she couldn't relax and let go, not even in paradise, with the woman she loved, by her side.

Said woman being currently angry at her, and probably for a reason.

Chapter Eight

"Joanna! What do you need?"

The voice on the other end of the line sounded terse, worried, but ready to deal with whatever crisis needed dealing with. For the first time since she'd made the decision, Joanna felt some relief.

"It's not what you think. I was hoping you could help me with some information. We're not in immediate danger, at least I don't think we are. I want to be on the safe side...and I wanted to hear your voice." The last part didn't come out like the joke she had meant to make. Joanna could imagine Vanessa shaking her head.

"You're not one to exaggerate. What kind of information?"

"We had a situation here. One guest's wife turned out to be a trafficked woman. Another one recognized her. Now the guy is dead, and the one who ID'd the wife is missing. Rue identified the men who shot him, and I'm afraid they might come back for her."

"What can we do?" Vanessa's friend Nick had warned her to never call the number unless they needed immediate relocation.

"I want Rue out of here as long as they still might be in the area. And I'm not sure about the local police. They didn't seem to be interested in delivering me or Rue to the authorities back home, but someone suggested they might be compromised."

"Whoa. I don't know who that someone is, but I don't think their information is good."

"What makes you think that?"

"There was a corruption scandal a few years ago, and they cleaned it up. I'm sure they're doing whatever they can to find that woman."

Joanna wondered what made Vanessa so sure.

"You don't think we would have sent you there if we weren't certain?"

Vanessa sounded hurt, so Joanna didn't point out that they'd been operating on a tight timetable—or that there was no such thing as a one hundred percent guarantee. She could see Vanessa's point though. She didn't do anything halfway.

"Okay. What about Rue?"

"We can arrange that if it's really necessary. What does she say about it?"

"It's not up for negotiation."

Vanessa was silent long enough for Joanna to start fidgeting.

"You know what it could mean?"

"I do. I also remember what happened last time."

"Last time we were dealing with a deranged serial killer."

"This time we are dealing with deranged men who sell women into domestic labor and sexual slavery. I'm not going to argue."

"No," Vanessa said.

For the second time tonight, Joanna wondered if she was speaking in riddles.

"No? I thought the number was for emergencies. This is one."

"We can look into all of it and send you additional security if necessary. But as long as Rue is with you, she'll be safer than anywhere else. Unless this is some relationship stuff you messed up. Then I can't help you."

Had she? Sometimes there was no warning when something good and reliable turned into a catastrophe. Her mother had hugged her in the morning, made her breakfast, and when Joanna returned home, she was gone forever. She couldn't trust. Before Rue, no one had ever given her a good reason.

"The woman who was forced to play the wife. She came to us seeking help. She thinks there might be a dirty cop reporting back to her captors. I know you think the worst of me when it comes to relationships, but I'm not making this up!"

"I never said you were. Just for the record, the person who has always thought the worst of you, is you, Joanna. I'll get back to you. Until then, talk to no one, and do nothing about this, okay? Best case scenario, we can all go back to our lives."

Joanna had barely clicked the End Call button when the scream jolted her into action.

⁂

The picture wasn't an exact replica of her memory, but together, the elements were enough to create a night terror worse than anything Rue had experienced in weeks. Short's face blending into the ones of the men she'd seen in the hallway, then Farrell's. Blood everywhere.

For long painful moments she wasn't sure if she was going to throw up, but fortunately the impulse abated, and Rue could breathe again. Joanna knew what to do, when to speak to her softly, and when it was safe to touch. One time, she had nearly punched her. The moves she'd learned from Zach had been slipping into her subconscious as much as the bad stuff. It could be a dangerous combination.

"It's okay. You're okay."

She collapsed in Joanna's embrace, only faintly aware of the light in the doorway. On soft footsteps, Alexandra walked away, giving them privacy again.

Rue realized that she'd likely woken her too.

"I'm sorry I didn't tell you about talking to my parents."

It seemed like the logical order to get that out of the way first. The statement surprised Joanna enough to halt the calming motion of her hand in Rue's hair, for a few seconds, before she resumed it.

"That's all right. We'll figure it out. There's something I have to tell you, too."

"I'm not going," Rue said, her voice firmer that she thought herself to be capable. "You've made your point. I know you're worried about me, but these people might be far away already. The man who's still on the run, he's every bit as much a loose end as I am. I gave the police a vague description. I'm sure he knows a lot more. They'd take care of him first, and he probably knows that."

"I'm...impressed. But Rue..."

"I'm not sure you heard me. There's nothing more to talk about. I choose to stay. Unless you got tired of me and want me gone, that is. I'm not going to overstay my welcome."

"There's no way you could. You're not making this easy."

Joanna kissed her, softly at first, then with a need that was familiar and comforting to Rue. Yes, they had a guest who had already walked into their bedroom without knocking earlier. She wasn't going to hear screams this time. They had to be quiet.

Rue wasn't surprised to find Alexandra already up when she walked into the kitchen.

"I thought I'd make myself useful," Alexandra commented. "Would you like a coffee?"

"You didn't have to do that." Rue found she couldn't be grumpy after last night's victory. The night terror had cost her a lot of energy, but then she'd spent more in a much more pleasant way. The memory made her shiver with bliss. "But I'd love to have one, thank you."

"There you go." Alexandra handed her a cup, her brief, knowing smile gone quickly. "I know you're not happy I'm here. I'm sorry."

"It's not you," Rue hurried to say. "It's assholes like him. If it wasn't for him, we wouldn't have to deal with this mess right now."

Alexandra didn't dispute her comment though the same might not be true for her.

"I'm glad you are here...and okay, considering. But regardless of any danger, we need to talk to somebody else who can help you more."

"A therapist?" Alexandra laughed bitterly as if that was an outlandish suggestion.

"Yes. And someone who can assist you in finding a job and a safe place to live."

"Good to have friends in high places."

"It doesn't hurt."

"What happened to you?"

The question startled Rue even though she should have expected it, from someone who could easily see through her defenses.

"Does it matter? He's dead." They had more in common than one might think.

"You survived. That's all that matters. I'm sorry to be nosy, though. It's none of my business, but...I had those nightmares sometimes. Before, they beat us when that happened. Harry, he wanted to make it better. He wasn't the worst."

Rue didn't know what to say that wouldn't sound patronizing or bitchy, so she said nothing. Joanna's timing was perfect as she joined them in the kitchen.

"I have good news for you," she said, smiling.

Rue realized they'd never talked about what Joanna wanted to tell her the night before.

<hr>

"No, absolutely not. I'll go away if you want me to, but I won't be talking to the police. I have nothing to tell them."

"As far as they are concerned, you are missing. I can assure you my friend is trustworthy, but they could charge you with faking a crime. Frankly, they could see us as accomplices. Right now, we can go and explain. The longer we wait, the more difficult this is going to get."

Alexandra made a sound that was close to a snort. Rue didn't think that "difficult" was a term enough to impress her.

"Is she going to vouch for every single cop on the island?"

"Well, there aren't so many to begin with," Rue said. Hearing that Vanessa was involved made her feel somewhat better. And worse. She was sure Joanna hadn't told her everything, not because she wanted to lie, but because she didn't want to air their unsolved issues in front of Alexandra. "I can't imagine she made that promise lightly. Besides, if they aren't looking for you too, that might give them more resources to find Tamara."

"Wait until tonight, please?"

Rue could tell that Joanna was just as perplexed by the request or rather wondering what difference a few hours would make. She connected the dots the moment Alexandra said, "I haven't decided anything in many months. Can we wait until tonight?"

"Yes. Sure, we can."

There was a time when Joanna hadn't felt torn between the questionable sense of duty, and the longing to leave it all behind. Leaving Alexandra alone at the house worried her, but there was no way she'd let Rue go to therapy by herself. The next best solution was to take Alexandra and wait with her in the car until after Rue was done.

This was their vacation. They had nothing else to do, right?

Joanna still didn't know how she could be so sure, but Vanessa had indeed insisted that the island's police force was trustworthy. Vanessa's word was good enough. It had to be.

Her warnings rang in Joanna's head as well. She wasn't on track to do something stupid. The police would protect Alexandra if need be, find resources for her. They would find the other man. End of story.

She turned to Alexandra, a bit startled when she realized the young woman was wearing Rue's clothes. Her mind had been on so many other things earlier, she hadn't even noticed.

Her gaze followed Alexandra's as she watched a family with two children, all of them holding ice cream cones. The longing in Alexandra's gaze was unmistakable.

"You'd like some ice cream? We have about half an hour left. There's a stand across the street."

"I've been eating enough of your food," Alexandra said, her tone wistful.

"Come on. What flavor?"

"You choose. Thank you."

Joanna crossed the street in brisk steps. There was a short line at the ice cream stand, but she could see Alexandra from her point of view. Only a few other cars sat in the parking lot of the therapist's building, mostly doctors and patients.

When it was her turn, she ordered for Alexandra and herself and handed the man on the truck a handful of change. Joanna turned around to see the car door open. The vehicle was empty.

"There you go," she said, handing the cones to the kids behind her, before she sprinted to the other side of the street.

Alexandra was gone.

Had she run because she wasn't ready to talk to the police? Joanna looked around herself, then back into the car, finding nothing that could have given her any clues as to Alexandra's whereabouts.

She entered the lobby, heading straight to a couple sitting across from the doorway.

"Have you seen a young woman come in, blonde, early twenties?" At least she still conveyed some authority. They both looked up from their cell phones, shaking their heads. Predictable. Joanna headed for the public toilets, startling a woman standing at the mirror as she barged in, checking every stall.

"Alexandra, if you're in there, please, let's talk about this."

In the mirror, she could see the woman giving her a strange look.

"Did you see someone come in? A young woman, about 5'7, blonde hair?"

"No," was the only reaction.

Back in the lobby, she found all elevators running, so she turned and took the stairs up to Dr. Shepherd's office. She jogged the last few steps, almost running into one of the doctors. Shepherd's office was at the end of the corridor, and as she came closer, she could hear disconcerting sounds, then a grunt.

Joanna attempted to kick the door, but it wouldn't budge. She tried again, putting her whole weight into the move this time, suppressing a yelp when her shoulder made contact with the unyielding wood. She did it again, not stopping until the door fell open and she nearly stumbled into the room.

Her jaw dropped when she saw Rue standing over the man, Dr. Shepherd a few steps away holding a statue that looked massive.

Alexandra was nowhere to be seen.

"I see you don't really need me here," she said, trying to sound nonchalant. She noticed Rue giving her a concerned look.

"Are you okay?" Rue asked.

"No. I don't think I am."

Chapter Nine

R ue felt strangely exhilarated at being able to put her newly learned skills to use. Every once in a while, she came to realize that the situation could have gone many different ways, none of them good for her, or Alexandra, or Dr. Shepherd.

But between her skills and the massive statue she had often admired on the shelf, Persephone, who had returned from the underworld, they managed to control the situation.

The man didn't know what hit him.

She hadn't frozen this time.

Having to talk to the police once more stifled her enthusiasm, reminding her of what didn't go right. Alexandra.

"We don't have to mention Alexandra," Joanna whispered to her as if reading her mind.

Rue shook her head. "We don't have to say that she spent the night, but we have to tell them she was here. She told the guy how to find me. Under duress, I'm sure, but the result's the same. Believe me, it's safer for everyone if the police can locate her, and she answers their questions."

"I should have never taken my eyes off her. Damn it."

"It's not your fault."

She could tell Joanna wasn't convinced but held back a response when the woman detective they'd met the other day came inside to greet them.

"I want to say, good to see you again, but I'm not sure the circumstances warrant that. I'm glad you're okay."

"We are. But I'm wondering how you couldn't know this man was still on the island." *Ouch.* She probably shouldn't have said that, judging from the detective's gaze, somewhere in between surprised and offended. The adrenaline was wearing off, and she felt herself starting to tremble.

Some things didn't add up. Alexandra had obviously been afraid, but there might be some things she hadn't told them.

Not that Rue could blame her. She and Joanna had kept secrets between them, some of them from the police.

"We're glad we could apprehend him now. What happened here?"

"He came barging in, with Alexandra in tow."

"Did he have a weapon?"

"Not that I know," Rue said. "Alexandra had a gun. He told her to, to shoot Dr. Shepherd, and me." She swallowed hard. The euphoria had been short-lived. "She was crying, didn't want to do it. He said, you did it before—with a gendered slur I don't want to repeat."

"All right." The detective's voice and gaze had softened.

"He was probably lying, or if he wasn't, they forced her," Joanna added. Rue had thought the same.

"Yes, I'm aware. What did you do?"

"I wish I could be clear about this, but at some point...My body just moved. I was fairly sure Alexandra didn't want to shoot anyone, but the longer she hesitated, the more likely it was he'd take the gun and do it himself. I just reacted. Turns out that worked."

Joanna looked like she was going to faint. She might be in pain from her encounter with that door or still absorbing what had happened in the span of minutes.

"Well, thank you for this. Now that we have the two of them, plus the evidence in Mr. Farrell's murder, you made our jobs a lot easier."

"Happy to help. Can we go home now?"

"Just a minute," she said, closing the door of the office they were standing in. "I mean it, we're grateful for your help. And I want you to be careful."

"What it is you're saying?" Joanna's eyes narrowed. "Is this a threat?"

Rue held her breath. It wouldn't be fair, after everything they'd been through, to find out that Vanessa had been wrong.

"Far from it. Inspector Young instructed me to tread carefully with your information, and I can assure you we have to the best of our abilities. So, we ask you to do the same and lay low in case the press is trying to contact you. And in general. That's all."

"Thank you, Detective."

A few minutes later, they sat in the car, the magnitude of recent events still catching up to them.

"All those lessons with Zach paid off," Joanna said eventually. "I can't even begin to imagine..." She pulled Rue into an embrace, but it was Rue who felt the warm wetness of tears against her neck.

"He said to channel my anger. I haven't always done it so well, but I guess...I did okay." Joanna held her tighter in answer.

"More than okay."

"You don't have to do all of it."

Joanna kissed her softly before she straightened and took a deep breath.

"I think we should go home," she said.

❧

"I'm sorry, but I can't give you that extra day off." Denise looked believably sorry. "With all that press, we got more bookings in advance than ever before. People are freaking morbid. I really need you two."

"What can you offer in return?" Joanna asked lazily. They had retreated to the inn's restaurant for dinner, and a few cocktails were doing wonders to take the edge off this day. As long as she didn't dig too deep. What would that do for Rue's therapy, to have her and the therapist threatened in what was supposed to be a safe space? Would Rue be able to find comfort in the fact that she'd been able to defend that space? Had the man taken Alexandra from the car, or had she lied to them, and met with him for some reason?

The police had found Tamara locked in a dingy apartment, hungry and dehydrated.

Once again, she pushed the questions away.

"Well, if you want, stay here overnight. A nice room with a view, a private Jacuzzi…"

"That sounds…Tempting. Why?"

Denise gaze was haunted. "All of those bookings, because a crime happened here. It's freaking me out. You did a lot more than your share, so…Consider it me showing my appreciation. I hope that we can all go back to normal."

No one needed to say out loud how much Joanna and Rue shared that hope. She wished that Alexandra and Tamara would be able to find some peace too.

※

Mixing pain meds with alcohol probably wasn't the best idea, but how many more bad things could happen? Dangerous question, Joanna thought as she lay in the king-size bed, aware of the faint throbbing in her shoulder. Endorphins, cocktails, and the meds had done the trick and dulled it down to a bearable level.

She watched Rue coming out of the bathroom, her gaze trailing over Joanna's naked body. Not a lot had happened since they'd retreated to the suite, the two of them too tired to do anything but lie in each other's arms under the fan.

Looking at Rue now, she felt an urgency, the weight of recent emotions crashing down on her.

"I'm sorry," she choked out.

Rue took off her robe, climbed onto the bed and lay next to her. "That's just the alcohol talking. You have nothing to be sorry about."

"I almost sent you away."

"For my protection. Granted, it was a bad idea, but you came to that conclusion already. I think you realized you have some use for me."

"That was silly. I don't know that I could be without you. I don't even know who I am without you anymore."

"Smooth. How could anyone top that?"

Joanna had an idea how she could take it even one step further, but if she did it now, Rue would think a close call and alcohol had fueled her thinking. No, the time wasn't yet right for *that*. Perhaps something else, something easier, now that they'd gotten a bit of rest, and couldn't sleep anyway.

"I like you on top," she said, not sorry or embarrassed that her voice revealed raw desire and need. She'd been in the cold for so long, and Joanna was aware that much of it had been her own doing. No more. Whatever happened, Rue kept her in the sunlight.

Rue didn't need any more prompting.

"You did great," Zach told her, and Rue beamed under the praise. "Now don't get cocky."

"What? I took out a guy a lot bigger than me. I have reason to be cocky."

"There's never a reason for that. Be proud. Move on. You still have a lot of work to do."

Rue barely kept herself from pouting. It was the last thing she wanted to hear—that the work was never done. That the nightmares might never go away completely, that a flashback could attack her without warning. No matter how much bliss she found in her life with Joanna, there would always be the work. Because there would always be violent, ignorant assholes.

"See, that's what I mean," Zach told her, satisfied, when she near collapsed by the end of her workout—but was still standing. "Now be proud. Next time will be better."

"I hate you," she gasped.

"I know, but that's okay. Have a great day, Rue."

"You too."

After a quick shower, Rue returned to the office for the first day after her vacation. The time hadn't been as restful as she might have hoped, but she didn't hate coming here either.

Working closely with Denise, she often marveled at having a work environment that she'd thought of as unattainable for most of her career. Denise didn't pay as much as Lawrence Mitchell, Joanna's father, had.

In exchange, Rue didn't have to tap dance around her and hide part of who she was. He hadn't fired her when she'd told him about her relationship with Joanna that had outed her at the same time, but he had revealed a side of him that was worse than what she already knew. Smiling and ignoring it was no longer an option.

Rue focused on the numbers in front of her. Numbers, math, distance from the emotions that inevitably came with going back to that week were her saving grace.

"It's so good to have you back." Denise sighed at her over-flowing email inbox. "Let's hope that none of the people that booked us for the next few months are criminals."

"Let's hope," Rue agreed.

Chapter Ten

E ven though people made that assumption from time to
time, Joanna hadn't been especially handy in her younger
years. Many of the skills that secured a roof over her head these
days came from her time in prison, when she'd gone to classes
purely to stop the thoughts in her head. She had learned enough
to assess what she could do, and when she had to call in electri-
cians and other contractors.

She hadn't always shown the same judgment when it came to
getting involved with police work long after she had to turn in
her shield—but that was over now, wasn't it?

Lay low, let the experts do their job. She could do that, especially when she was still black and blue on one side due to that
damn door. Rue had handled things on the other side of it just
fine.

She was done fixing the bathroom tile of the empty room
that would soon be booked. As she walked outside, her gaze on
the view of the green around them, the ocean in the distance,
Joanna truly understood what she'd gained, and almost lost
again.

She wasn't sorry for helping the women best she could.

She was starting to realize that she was allowed to take care of
herself too.

Lawrence Mitchell frowned at the taste of his coffee and sighed to no one in particular. He missed Rue, not that he'd ever admit it out loud to anyone. He was on the third assistant since she'd been gone. The first to replace her was a young man, then a woman, now a recent graduate named Bill Meyers held the job. All from great schools, none of them showing great promise.

Rue had been the perfect assistant in his opinion. She kept things running without bothering him every five minutes, had a sixth sense for when he didn't want to take any calls or visitors, and she knew how to make his coffee.

Too bad he'd been so wrong about her, and it took him so long to realize that not only did she support Joanna's problem, but she shared it. It was for the better, her being gone, and Joanna too.

When the police had come to talk to him, he lied about when he'd last seen his daughter. He was all for her enjoying her life, as long as it was out of his sight, and without his money. Her being locked up again would only mean bad press for the company.

Uttering a swear word he'd deny ever using, he got up to make his own coffee.

That was Joanna's fault too.

Lucky didn't even begin to describe it. Even on a work night, they could go down to the beach and have dinner nearby, in time to watch the sun set.

"Do you still miss your old life?" Rue asked.

"Which one?" It wasn't even a joke. The longer they stayed here, the clearer things had become to Joanna. Part of her would always be the same. And then there were parts she was happy to leave behind, but she guessed it wasn't what was on Rue's mind. "The answer is no. Whatever I might have been able to have before, I couldn't have this. I am grateful for what Vanessa, and probably Theo, did for us. I can't keep looking back, and I don't think they are. What about you?"

"I thought about your dad today," Rue admitted.

"Better you than me."

Someone might say that sounded harsh, but Rue understood the context better than anyone else. There was not a soul in Lawrence's private or business environment that didn't describe him as polite, soft-spoken, old-fashioned in a charming way. It wasn't until her mid-twenties that Joanna had overcome the gaslighting.

"He never once raised his voice at me. Until the day I revealed to him that I was your lesbian lover, of course."

Joanna nearly choked on her sip of water. "You told him that?" She couldn't remember that term from the first time Rue had told her the story.

"Not in those words, no." Rue laughed. "But the gist was the same." More serious, she continued. "He's really like so many people, they fool themselves thinking toeing the line is something to admire as long as you do it in a polite tone and good clothes. The worst is I was starting to tell myself it was all right to keep working there as long as I didn't believe in the same things."

"We're both better off." Without him in our lives. Joanna didn't say it out loud. She didn't have to.

"I am proud of you," Rue said. "Of the person you became in spite of him."

81

The surge of emotion caught her off guard. Typical for her, Joanna had to think of the days waking up to an empty bottle and a half-filled ash tray on the table, and inconsequential hook-ups, one of them turning out to be a sadistic criminal. She blamed her father for a lot, but not those things. She had brought them on herself.

"No, don't go there. You saved my life. And Alexandra's. No one can really say how many women were saved because Decker and Short don't walk the earth anymore. I've seen the places Lawrence gives money to, and I think it's unfair that he sleeps fine at night. We have to say these things at some point."

"I agree. I wasn't aware we would say them in public." Joanna stole an untouched napkin from an empty neighboring table to wash her face.

"I'm sorry about that. And I wanted to say that I have no more secrets. I told my parents that we'll be busy in the next few weeks. Laying low, right?"

"Yes, we can do that."

That night, for the first time, Joanna played the piano for Rue, wondering if she hadn't turned out like her father at all, what it was her mother had given her. She didn't miss the life she'd had any longer, but a small part of her still imagined the life she might have had if her mother had taken her with her that day.

⁓

Denise hadn't promised too much: In the following weeks, all of them worked overtime, along with every single one of the inn's employees. The room in which Farrell and Alexandra had stayed was popular.

Joanna wasn't surprised or particularly bothered, only confirmed in her perception of most people. She was lucky to have encountered some good ones—like Vanessa and Theo, Denise, Rue's parents.

And most of all, Rue.

In the midst of the hectic activity, one of the shuttle drivers had a minor accident in his private vehicle, so Denise asked Joanna to take over his route to the airport.

"I know that's not normally your job, but I'm sorry, I'm really backed up here."

"No problem. I'm on it." There was no way Joanna could say no though she preferred her usual odd jobs, the ones she was often able to do when there was no one around. It was different when she and Rue spent time at the restaurant or the bar sometimes—they blended in with the other guests. This was more contact than Joanna would have liked, but given the problem, there was no alternative. It had been quiet for a while. This shouldn't be any different.

It was an especially hot day on the island, making Joanna grateful for the air conditioning in the shuttle. The drive was an easy one, get a group of visitors to the airport and pick up the arriving ones in the area that had been marked in their booking confirmation. Except for the area close to the airport, there was little traffic, and the only interruption was a herd of sheep on occasion.

On day three, Joanna had lost her concern. The people she was driving weren't much interested in conversations, groups of women and men, couples, families, all mostly occupied with themselves.

On day five, she picked up a couple of women and two men from the airport. One of the men was older, in his sixties, the other guests closer in age, early thirties perhaps. At first, Joanna had thought that they were together, but the man took a seat next to her in the front—without asking. The women sat in the bench in the back, talking to each other in hushed tones.

"How long is it to the inn?" the older man asked.

"Not long. About twenty minutes."

Joanna saw the other man smile to himself. She wondered what was so amusing about that.

"You'll have time to check in, and there'll be a welcome cocktail for you after," she informed the shuttle's occupants. She had said the same sentence so often this week, it was starting to lose any meaning.

"That sounds great," the man next to her said. "What time are you off work?"

"Not at that time," Joanna returned, keeping a polite smile in place.

It wasn't the first time a guest had come on to her, but since she kept her distance, it didn't happen all that often. It was far too early, not that there was ever a right time for it.

In the mirror, she could see the women's expressions, interest laced with irritation. She wondered if he had bothered them too. They might have to keep an eye on him, just in case.

"That's too bad. What about tomorrow?"

"Planes land and take off every four hours. You do the math."

"Touché. You must forgive me. I step off the plane and this place...It tastes like freedom."

Perhaps he had already started on the cocktails during the flight.

"Well, I hope you will all enjoy it," Joanna said. It didn't mean a thing that her skin was crawling. She just didn't like his type. Part of a bigger problem, just like her father.

Rue had been right. She was allowed to be proud.

⁂

In the course of the afternoon and early evening, Joanna forgot about the annoying guest, until after a long shower and a change of clothes she reunited with Rue.

He sat at the counter with a woman, but turned and waved to her when she walked in.

"Who's that?" Rue asked before she got up to kiss Joanna in greeting.

"Just some guest from earlier. He wanted to know if I'd have the welcome cocktail with him. I guess he got over it that I didn't. How was your day?"

"Long, but since it didn't involve him, I guess I can't complain. What would you like to drink?"

Rue already half-turned into the direction of the bar.

"A beer, please. Thank you."

"Be right back."

Joanna watched her walk up to the counter, chatting with the bartender for a bit. Her gaze fell back on the man who was studying the interaction rather than his companion. She wasn't anyone Joanna had driven this week, so she had to have been at the inn for a while. Her body language didn't scream discomfort. Maybe she was hiding it well, and maybe there truly was a match for everyone. Edward Short and Grace Lester had been a perfect match made in hell.

It was hard not to think of them at all. Joanna and Rue needed to build a new life from the ashes because they had burned it all down. Well, neither Grace nor Edward lived on a beautiful island.

Rue returned with two beers, a slice of lime sticking out of each bottle.

"I couldn't help but overhear a part of their conversation," she said. "I don't think he's going to bother you anymore. They made plans for tonight."

"Good."

"What is it?"

Joanna sent the slice of lime down the neck of the bottle, watching the foam rise.

"Sometimes I wish I could see the world like normal people. Less cynical."

"It's hard not to be cynical once you've learned some things," Rue admitted. "But us, here, that's only the first step. Everything is still so fresh, not to mention that someone was murdered here."

"When I was twenty years younger, I would have shrugged it off. Now the kind just makes me sick."

"Not every jerk is a serial killer. There would be few people around."

"I love your use of logic."

"I'm glad. It would be questionable as a sense of humor."

Joanna turned her chair so that the couple at the bar wasn't in her line of sight any longer.

"So, tell me more about your day."

Despite the odd start, that guest didn't try to talk to her during his stay. Rue saw him a couple of times with the other woman, and they seemed to have hit it off.

Perhaps she'd been overestimating herself, Joanna thought when she drove the shuttle bus to the front of the hotel.

"Oh, it's you," he said before climbing in next to her. "I haven't seen you around much."

"That's because I've been working."

"You live close by?"

"I do," she said, unwilling to give him any more information. Perhaps he'd been drinking the last time. Perhaps he was awkward with women and had found one who didn't mind—even better. All she wanted was to drop him off at the airport.

The older man who had arrived on the same day, came to join them, and according to Joanna's list, this ride was complete. The younger women were staying another week.

"Off we go," she said, fastening her seatbelt after she'd put the man's suitcase in the back. "I hope you enjoyed your stay."

Next to her, the man whose name was Liam Preston, leaned back in his seat, closing his eyes. "Like you wouldn't imagine."

He might not be one of the worst, but he still came across as a creep, even to Joanna who had often been the only woman in otherwise all male groups. She was glad he'd be off the island in a few hours.

***

His research had taken him to many fascinating places, giving him a lot to think about while he worked on the next steps. He never lost sight of his priority though: Two women who had tried to make their mark in a men's world, attracted by danger. He had a clear vision of what he wanted to do for, and with, each of them. For that, he had to figure out more pieces of the puzzle, investigate the players.

Like the surprisingly rich friend and her connections. All those connections had led to a trail, the story of two other women, trafficked from Eastern Europe, who had escaped their fate.

He leaned back in his chair, drinking from his beer, a smile appearing on his face when he watched the video. It had been taken with a cell phone and uploaded to the Internet in a place where few people would think to look...But he wasn't "few people."

Cops were arresting a man who had bought a wife for himself.

He shook his head at the stupidity. It didn't work like that. Women needed to be coaxed, offered a valuable alternative. He paused the video and studied the frozen image.

He had made his choice.

He knew what she wanted more than anything, and he was going to provide it for her.

She'd be forever at his mercy.

Chapter Eleven

L iam Preston, or at least that's what he was going with these days, had indeed enjoyed his trip, even though it was more of a research venture than a vacation. Lucky for the women and one man he had pursued during his stay. His focus wasn't on them.

Back home, it didn't take him long to put all the puzzle pieces together and work on the logical next step.

The building was busy as always, no one noticing a thirty-something man in a suit. No one noticed that he'd been here before, with a visitor's badge under a different name.

Now he wore Bill Meyers'. Poor Bill was probably still frantically searching for his this morning, wondering what had happened the night before after too many drinks with a stranger. He probably didn't even remember how much he'd told that stranger about his boss.

Liam kept his head down as he headed straight for his destination. He had a window of a few minutes. The secretary would be on her coffee break, the personal assistant...Well, he wouldn't be available today. He had learned from Bill that Mitchell would be there. On his agenda he had a meeting with one of his fiercest competitors.

For the last two floors, Liam took the stairs to be on the safe side, and he entered through the main door of the company's offices with Bill's key card. It was quiet up here, reeking of obscene wealth. Not that he had anything to say against it. His time as a freelancer had brought him considerable financial security.

Now he was just killing for fun.

He confirmed what he'd observed before: The secretary's desk was empty. Liam believed in a polite start for every interaction, no matter how messy things might have to get down the line. He knocked. There was no answer. He tried again.

"Damn it, I told you no interruptions—"

When Liam walked into the room, the man who had yelled from the other side of the door, jumped to his feet with surprising speed.

"Who the hell are you?"

Politeness ended right here. Liam laughed at Lawrence Mitchell's anger. He moved quickly and punched the older man. Again. And again. He only spoke a few words.

When he was satisfied with his work, Liam wiped his gloved hands on the handkerchief he'd brought. He carefully closed the office door on his way out and stuffed both gloves and handkerchief into a small backpack. He left the building whistling. The plan was in motion.

Lawrence Mitchell was lucky, though he didn't feel that way when he came to on the floor of his office, bleeding onto the expensive carpet. Part of him was surprised he wasn't dead, and for several seconds, the anger and terror threatened to overwhelm him.

How could this have happened? Certainly, he had angered some people in his career, bleeding heart liberals like Rue and his daughter, but these folks usually didn't revert to means like this...

The thought of Joanna made him uneasy before he understood why, and then the memory hit him.

"Bill!" he cried, before he remembered that Bill Meyers hadn't come in today. Instead, his secretary came rushing in, her hand going to her mouth when she saw what happened.

"Don't just stand there," he hissed. "Go get the police and get me Detective Kato on the phone."

He had to correct the record...and get rid of the disturbing taste of blood. Even so he was likely to miss that damn meeting. Grant would not be happy, but at the moment, Lawrence couldn't care less.

⁂

Detective Allison Kato had an instinct for when someone wasn't telling her the whole truth. That made her good at her job. In the past few months, it had also put her in a state of constant frustration, because she had no choice but to live with half-truths and missing information.

Edward Short was dead. Grace Lester remained behind bars.

Joanna and Rue had ridden off into the sunset, wherever that was. Vanessa Young had left Internal Affairs, and that left Allison and Theo back at work, pretending that with the Short/Lester case closed, there weren't any inconsistencies left.

The outcome wasn't a bad one by any means, from a pragmatic or human standpoint. She had other cases to worry about. She didn't know the whole story, and that bothered her. When she came to work that morning, Allison had no idea that an hour later, she would be sitting next to Lawrence Mitchell's hospital bed, hearing the words that sent her into a disturbing tailspin of doubt.

"He said, your daughter says hello," Mitchell insisted.

Allison didn't know Mitchell or his daughter well, but she could vouch for one thing—Joanna's single-minded determination for saving victims, one in particular. Allison had met Mr. Mitchell only once before. He and Joanna didn't talk. He had rejected her for being a lesbian a long time ago. As far as Allison knew, they hadn't seen each other in years. This didn't make sense.

"Are you sure? This was a traumatic situation…"

"I'm not stupid or deaf," he shot back at her. Father and daughter might be at odds, but Allison could see where Joanna got that stubbornness from. Also, she realized that he was offended by the idea that anything could faze or frighten him.

"I didn't imply either one, Mr. Mitchell. Do you have any idea what he could have meant?"

"If I did, don't you think I would tell you? I gave you a description. Find that son of a bitch. And find Joanna."

"You don't think…She had anything to do with this?" As she said it out loud, the mere idea sounded ridiculous to Allison.

"Until today, I would have said it's impossible, but she does blame me for a lot of the bad things in her life. And she came to threaten me in case I did anything to interfere with her precious girlfriend's career. Not that I had any interest in doing so, and that's what I told her."

This was getting more confusing by the second.

"Rue?"

"Yes, of course Rue. From what I hear, she's disappeared. I can assure you that wasn't my doing."

None of this made sense. Joanna had killed a man. Maybe two. Both were sadistic murderers who had abducted and tortured women. Joanna wouldn't associate with a violent individual, unless…Allison felt the blood drain from her face as the possibilities floated around in her mind.

Now she wished Theo was here. While the subject of Joanna seemed to be laden with regret and guilt over missed chances, he knew her. He knew what she was capable of and for what reasons.

"Get some rest, Mr. Mitchell," she said. "I'll get back to you when we have news."

⁂

Denise had hired an additional part-time driver, and so Joanna was mostly back to her normal work. Dr. Shepherd had moved into a different office. Everyone went back to their blessed routines.

No more visits from the police. Liam Preston, the creepy guest, was gone.

She and Rue could finally breathe.

That night, Joanna waited for her in the bar after her shift, chatting with the bartender. No one had heard from Alexandra or Tamara, but perhaps they could now find peace as well.

"That was something," Oliver said. "We've never had this many criminals and craziness around here. Usually it's a safe haven."

"Let's hope we can go back to that."

"I'm off now," he said, nodding to his replacement who had just come in. "How about we drink to that?"

"That Preston guy is finally gone?" Marika, Oliver's colleague asked. "I'll drink to that later. Boy, was he annoying."

Back off, Joanna reminded herself. Nothing to see here, at least not for her.

"He bothered you?"

"He bothered everyone," Marika scoffed. "Well, some didn't mind. He went off with a different person every night. Mostly women. One guy."

Oliver shrugged. "Well, as long as they all went willingly, that's fine with me. He was odd though."

If anything, Joanna was fairly relieved that everyone shared her impression, though the man wasn't their problem any longer.

"To safe havens," she said, raising her glass in a toast, the moment Rue entered the bar. She walked over to greet Joanna with a kiss.

"What are we celebrating?"

"Freedom."

She would have to admit that many of those ghosts she couldn't seem to let go of, she had created herself. Joanna vowed to do better, starting right now.

Chapter Twelve

A llison had lured Theo away from the station for a late
lunch. Her stomach was growling, though she was fairly
certain the subject matter she'd have to raise would spoil their
appetite.

Of course he knew about the intruder at Mitchell's.

"The description is out. I talked to Bill Meyers, the assistant,
but he has no idea how his keycard got into the wrong hands."

"It doesn't look like attempted murder to me," Theo commented. "More like someone was trying to send a message. You
think Mitchell told you the whole truth? Did he get involved
with some shady people and failed to pay? In any case, it sounds
like you've been making some progress. A description is good."

"Yeah...but...There's something I left out. I wanted to run it
by you first."

"Okay. I'm listening."

"It's about Joanna."

Theo sat up straighter in the booth. "Why? She and Mitchell
haven't talked in almost two decades."

"According to Mitchell, the guy told him, your daughter says
hello, in those exact words."

"What the fuck—"

Allison wasn't sure how to interpret Theo's outburst.

"You know her better than I do—"

"No way. There's no way in hell."

"He didn't always treat her well."

"He cut her off when she was in college. That's a pretty disgusting thing to do, but it's not a reason, all of a sudden, to send someone to beat him up."

"Unless cutting her off wasn't all he did, or there's something he did to Rue...We don't know where either of them is."

Theo shook his head. "Whoa, Al, stop it. You're way off."

"Do you know where she is?"

"No," he said, looking her straight in the eye. "Joanna made mistakes, and she's been through some rough times, but this isn't like her. For what it's worth, her old man's a homophobe and a sexist, which is bad enough, but I don't think he crossed the lines you think he crossed."

To Allison, his words sounded suspiciously rehearsed for someone who was learning this information for the first time. Still, it made sense, didn't it?

"Someone might be messing with him...and Joanna," she reasoned.

"Sounds like a theory. Once we find the guy, we'll figure it out."

"It would be helpful to talk to Joanna and Rue, though."

"Perhaps, but my money is still on Mitchell's business deals. A company with that net worth, there are bound to be skeletons in the closet."

Allison sipped her tea, thinking that she liked Theo's interpretation better. If anything, it left both Joanna and her father in a better light. It was tempting.

"Do you think she'd want to know? I mean he's her father, and this could have gone either way."

Theo picked up his burger. "That's a rather philosophical question. I'm thinking you overestimate how well I know her.

We worked together, and then it all went to hell. As far as I'm concerned, I hope she's happy."

Allison hadn't missed the fact that nothing he said disproved any of her theories.

What a mess. The sooner they found the man who had beaten up Lawrence, the better.

Case closed.

❦

They were getting ready for bed when the phone rang. Joanna was still half-naked in the bathroom hearing Rue pick up and speak to the caller quietly.

A moment later, there was a knock on the bathroom door. Joanna put on a robe and opened.

"It's Vanessa for you."

Rue looked pale, putting her on edge immediately. "What is it?"

"Your dad," Rue said, her solemn tone doing nothing to disperse Joanna's worries. She took the phone from her and sat on the edge of the bed.

"What's the matter?" she asked, expecting the worst. "Is he..."

"He's going to be okay," Vanessa said. "He's in the hospital right now, but I think they'll let him go this week."

"Heart attack?" It seemed the most logical explanation.

"Someone gained access to his office and beat him up."

Joanna sat, silent, as the seconds ticked by. This was a surprise, and a bad one at that. A person had to be savvy to get past Lawrence's security.

"I'm sorry to hear that." She assumed there was more, or Vanessa wouldn't have broken the rules.

"Yeah, me too. There's something..." Joanna was aware of Rue watching her with concern.

"The intruder said, your daughter says hello, to him...Joanna?"

"I'm here. That's..." Not possible, she wanted to say. She could only think of one person who might hate her enough to want to do this. Two, maybe, but Decker's wife had never contacted her after the trial, and she didn't know the kind of people for this job. Grace Lester...Joanna shuddered at the though of her. "How's Grace doing these days?" she asked.

"Better than she deserves, but I don't think she's in the position to orchestrate something like that."

"Stranger things have happened. My bet would be on her."

"Okay," Vanessa said. There was a whole world behind that word.

"Okay what? This is just going to get worse, isn't it? No one thinks I hired him, or do you? Look, I hate men who hurt women. I know what I did. But you know this is not...Vanessa, what the hell are you saying?"

Rue flinched at the raised tone of her voice.

"Allison has a theory that something could have sent you over the edge. Her words, not mine. Something that could have to do with his behavior towards Rue...or towards you, when you were a child. Again, I'm only repeating what I heard, and I wanted to share with you so we can do damage control best we can."

"We can do this quick. She's wrong on everything."

"Are you sure?"

"Yes, I am, but Theo's got to lean harder on Lester. If anyone wants to mess with my mind, it's her."

"Thanks." Joanna could hear the regret in Vanessa's voice. "I'm sorry I had to bring this up."

"Yeah, me too. I can understand why you did it though. Can we leave it at that or are you going to tell me there's a warrant out for me?"

"No. It's under control at the moment, and again, I'm sorry."

"How is he?" Joanna asked, sensing that Vanessa was about to end the call.

"Shocked, of course, though he tries to hide it and act tough. Allison says he looked pretty bad, but he had no life-threatening injuries."

"All right. Thank you." Joanna laid the phone aside and lay back on the bed. Rue curled up next to her.

"I'm sorry," she whispered.

"It will be okay. Just a bunch of bizarre coincidences. He'll be fine."

She wasn't sure if the same could be said for her, ever. Joanna hated the conflicting emotions this incident brought up. Of all the times she'd wished he would get over himself, she'd never wished anything like this on him. The more she thought about it, the more it made sense. Grace and Edward had always done their homework. She had to know. No one else had an interest in messing with her life this way...and judging from Allison Kato's reaction, it was working to some extent.

She had to trust Theo and Vanessa to do the right thing. Carry on.

It was all they could do.

⁂

Apparently, her mind needed refuge, and the vision was as perfect as it possibly could be, the dream wedding, Rue whispering, 'yes, of course', and in the first row, Rue's parents, Lawrence Mitchell and...Joanna woke with a start, self-conscious at the tears on her face. It was silly, impossible. She didn't even know what her mother looked like today, and for sure, neither she nor Lawrence would be present if they ever got married.

Joanna could think of a few friends she'd love to have at the occasion, though that wasn't a realistic option either. Denise and Oliver would likely be witnesses.

They could have a ceremony on the beach...She had to stop longing for something she could never have and start focusing on the amazing second—or third?—chance she'd been given.

Her inability to rest had nothing to do with Rue, or their new life not being enough. It was everything.

She might not be able to make peace with her parents' actions, before it was too late, but Joanna had lived with that knowledge for most of her life. It wasn't the reason for sleepless nights either.

Somewhere, someone, wouldn't let her be.

It had to be Grace, the woman with the most inappropriate name, who had crossed Joanna's path when she was at her lowest.

There was nothing Joanna could do, and it was driving her mad.

What would be her next move—since there was almost no doubt that there would be one? What was the end goal?

"Your thoughts are too loud," Rue murmured beside her, and before Joanna had a chance to apologize, she was on top of her. "Let me distract you?"

If anyone could make the hamster wheel in her head stop, it was Rue. As she let her kisses ignite her body, she flashed back to the part of the dream that had not made her cry, the part that had been complete bliss.

That part was real—regardless of whether they made it official or not. If their recent contacts with the police hadn't presented a problem, perhaps a marriage license wouldn't either? Joanna didn't know anymore, but whatever helped protect Rue, and their relationship, was something to consider.

She let herself go, safe in Rue's hands.

"I want to marry you," the words came tumbling out.

Rue barely paused in trailing kisses down her chest and stomach. For a moment. Joanna worried, that she hadn't heard her, or worse, that her proposal was premature.

"I want that too."

She shouldn't doubt her, ever. The perfect life was already here, no matter what happened, or who was there to witness it.

"Did you mean what you said earlier or was that just, I don't know, in the throes of passion?" Rue laughed at her own choice of words. It was contagious. And so easy to answer.

"I never say anything I don't mean. Especially not in that context."

Joanna stretched her toes in the warm sand and took a sip of her coffee. They had woken early and decided to have a breakfast picnic on the beach before going to work.

"We are so damn lucky. People come here for their honeymoon. For us, it's home."

"True."

"Do you think there's a way for my parents to attend?"

"I don't know, maybe. Anyone who wanted to find us probably would have already."

She wasn't sure what Vanessa and Theo had done, or the female detective they'd spoken to, but the people in charge seemed in agreement: Joanna and Rue hurt no one. There was no harm in leaving them alone. Easy, right?

"Would you want to tell your dad?" Rue asked softly.

"Why? There's no way he would come here. Not because the trip is long, 'mind you."

"I know, but maybe what happened..."

"Changed his mind? Vanessa didn't say it in so many words, but her sympathetic tone really came through. Detective Kato isn't the only person who thinks I might have hired the guy who attacked him. Okay, we went far off topic. This was supposed to be romantic."

Rue laid an arm around her shoulders. "It is. I'm sorry I brought this up. If my parents could come, it would be great, but if it's not possible, we'll make it work. And if it's safer to just have a ceremony, nothing official, we can do that too. This," Rue continued, indicating the ocean laid out in front of them, "isn't going away. We deserve it. We deserve to be safe."

One day, Joanna would believe it, though she still wondered if Theo had any luck getting information from Grace Lester.

⁓

"A wedding? That's awesome!" Denise hugged her tightly. "I think we're all overdue for some good news. Of course we can do it here on the property. Or on the beach, what do you think? Have you thought about dresses? Centerpieces?"

It was the first opportunity for Joanna to react since she'd entered Denise's office.

"To be honest, we haven't figured out much yet. I just wanted to give you a heads-up."

"I'm thrilled. Get going, I want this to happen as soon as possible."

"Okay, boss. I heard you."

Joanna hadn't told her anything about the attack on Lawrence. She wished him a speedy recovery, but that was all she could and wanted to do on her end.

Chapter Thirteen

A new office, the same people. Dr. Shepherd offered her a glass of water, and they sat down as usual, a soft breeze coming through the open window.

"How have you been?" Dr. Shepherd asked.

"Good." Rue didn't think she'd have to go into detail of last night. It was good for her to take charge, and for Joanna to let go, leaving some room for change in the roles they had adopted early on in their relationship. Joanna, the protector. Rue, the...She wasn't a victim any longer. She'd sworn she'd never be one again. The doctor and Zach had done a great deal to help her achieve that goal, but nothing had helped her heal like Joanna submitting to her touch. Joanna, her lover.

Rue had to smile, realizing all her thoughts seemed to go in one direction today. "I mean, we're back to work, it doesn't look like any criminals are about to barge in at any moment, and Joanna asked me to marry her. I said yes."

"That's great news." Dr. Shepherd smiled. "Let's come back to that in a moment. We haven't talked much about the incident."

"Why did you change your office?" Rue asked, genuinely curious.

"Better security. I didn't like the reminder." In the months they'd been working together, honesty proved to be the most important rule for their relationship. It was understood this was about Rue's process and healing...but Dr. Shepherd didn't tell her lies either. In fact, Rue had noticed she looked at her a different way.

Good.

Things were good.

"How did it feel?"

"Like I was allowed to be cocky and feel invincible for a moment?" Rue shook herself. "I'm aware that this could have gone so wrong, but it didn't. Now I know all that sweating at the gym wasn't for nothing."

"How did you integrate it with...?"

"The rest of the story? It changes the story," Rue said. "Sometimes you can't negotiate. Sometimes you have to hit first."

It hadn't been so clear before in her mind, and she was grateful for Dr. Shepherd providing a context in which she could get her thoughts in order. Rue had accepted what Joanna told her about the past, understood it on a philosophical level, in the context of justice. Much of the time she'd spent as Short's hostage was still a blur, with little memory of conscious decisions.

Now, Rue knew for sure. She didn't hesitate or falter. The man she'd fought was in custody, not dead, but she knew that she could do what needed to be done. Perhaps this was what she'd needed for peace.

"I hope Alexandra and Tamara are okay, wherever they are. I can't believe I was so petty to be...I don't know, almost jealous. I get it now."

"They are survivors. Like you."

"Yes. We were all lucky."

She included Dr. Shepherd in that statement, certain that the therapist was aware.

Grace Lester regarded her fingernails, looking bored.

Theo wasn't yet sure whether or not he was wasting his time with this visit—she sure thought he was wasting hers.

"Joanna who?" she said. "I don't know where you got the idea that I care about her. I'm doing all right, and they're all younger and prettier than her."

Did she want to taunt him, or Joanna, hoping he'd tell her?

"We can cut this short. Did you hire someone to beat up her father?"

Grace laughed. And laughed. It was so fake it made his skin crawl.

"I said something funny?"

"Indeed, you did, Detective. I'm not sure you're aware how prison works, but I don't get to hire anyone to do anything. Not on the outside, at least. In here I have some sway. What can I say? I have a lot to offer." She looked at him, a smile tugging at the corners of her lips. "Perhaps that's what you came here for? A little fantasy to bring back to your girlfriend?"

"I'm good, thanks. I see you're not going to tell me the truth, so I'll let you go back to whatever it is you can do in here." He gave her a smirk, aware of the flash of anger on her face, before she put the sweet smile back in place.

"That's so kind of you, Theo. Say hello to Joanna. I hope she's happy."

"Oh, she is, don't worry."

"So, someone went after her daddy. It wasn't me, but that is interesting. Perhaps next time they choose somebody she actually cares about?"

Already at the door, Theo made a sharp turn. "What the hell are you talking about?"

105

"Nothing. Just making conversation. *You* came to see *me*. I didn't do anything, but you seem to be out of theories. I gave you one. You're welcome."

He didn't answer, but left the room, more troubled than when he'd come in. In spite of her denial, Theo wasn't ready to rule out any involvement. Worse, unless Grace was playing games, everyone Joanna cared about could be in danger.

Including Vanessa.

He ordered the special evening menu, complete with different wines for each course. He sat close enough to have the man and woman in his sight, though he couldn't hear what they were saying. It wasn't important. Their worried gazes spoke volumes—and he was here to observe and have an excellent meal.

Liam knew that Vanessa Young and Theo Randolph didn't come to this restaurant often. Likely, they were stressed about recent events and felt the need to treat themselves. They better. Things were about to get worse for both of them.

He watched them interact, talk, and at some point, hold hands on the table, the gesture causing a sharp pang of envy. They didn't deserve to be together, flaunt their relationship, when he couldn't do the same.

Not yet anyway.

After dessert and coffee, he paid, leaving a hefty tip.

He walked past Theo and Vanessa's table, resisting the urge to tip over one of their glasses. He imagined, though, the dark read fluid spreading over the blush fabric of Vanessa's expensive dress. Would she shriek? Be angry?

Liam didn't have time to elaborate on his fantasy. He took a cab to an address two blocks from his destination. Then he walked up to the front door and knocked, gun in hand. When she answered, he fired two shots and walked away, to the car that was waiting in a parking lot down the street.

Execution Phase Two—done.

∼⌇∼

Theo and Vanessa had enjoyed sort of a working date night, discussing the progress in Mitchell's case, when Theo received a call. Allison knew he was with Vanessa tonight, so she wouldn't try to reach him if it wasn't important.

"It's bad," she said without preamble. "I know you have the night off, but you should be here."

"Where is that?" he asked, sensing that the quiet evening was over.

"Remember Nate Gibson? I'm at his place."

It took him a few seconds to make the connection. "The driver who found Christina Danvers." Danvers had escaped from the slasher, almost running into Gibson's truck. If it hadn't been for the man's quick intervention, she might not have survived.

Gibson was also a former colleague of Joanna's at the warehouse where she'd worked after her prison sentence.

"Don't tell me..."

"It's the wife. Two gunshot wounds to the chest. He came back home, found her as soon as he walked in. The door was unlocked."

Theo wanted to curse. Smash something. Neither option would be helpful to anyone. Another case, this time a murder carried out, once again connected to Joanna. Somebody didn't want her to live in peace.

And Grace Lester had made a chilling prediction.

"Didn't they have children?"

"They were upstairs, didn't hear anything. How soon can you get here?"

"I'll get a cab. See you there."

Theo turned to Vanessa, pained that there was nothing he could tell her to alleviate the fear in her eyes. Whoever the person behind these crimes was, they were escalating, and fast.

"I'll come with you," she said, already taking out her cell phone to call a cab.

Vanessa had changed into a job with the private sector, but she was still consulting with the department at times. More importantly, Theo didn't want to leave her alone. He didn't share that reason, but he was sure she was aware.

Nate Gibson had called his sister who was now with the two terrified children. As soon as they were out of sight, his voice broke.

"Who the hell would do something like this?"

Vanessa stayed in the background, let Theo and Allison do their jobs, though she had some answers for him. Someone with no conscience. No soul. Someone who wanted to make Joanna suffer all over again. By proxy, this concerned her too, because she was the one who had thrown the book at Joanna all those years ago.

It was too late to obsess about what if's.

This person had beaten and killed people related to Joanna, and chances were, they had other names on their list.

"Allison, can I talk to you for a second?"

Joanna and Rue had started their meal with champagne on the house, promising Denise to take her various suggestions into consideration. It wasn't until they were home that Joanna noticed the missed calls.

Many of them, all from Vanessa.

No. No more bad news, not now. Couldn't they have five minutes to plan the most important day of their lives? She didn't want to hear that her father had died from complications. No matter how small he'd tried to make her feel, and sometimes succeeded, she'd still grieve him. She didn't want to, but that wasn't up to her.

"Maybe it's not that bad," Rue said, laying a hand on her arm. It was only for Joanna's benefit, and they both knew it. What didn't kill her hadn't made her that much stronger, she thought.

"Well, let's get it over with."

The moment Vanessa picked up, she said, "This is about Lawrence, right? I knew it. I'm sorry you're the one who had to tell me—"

"Joanna, no. Your dad is fine."

Kira, she thought. Or something happened to Rue's parents, and she wanted to tell me first?

"Oh, okay. Be gentle, okay? We're planning our wedding."

"Joanna, that's wonderful." The sadness in her tone didn't bode for anything good.

"It is, even though you're about to hit me with something less wonderful. All right. Do it."

"Joanna, Nate Gibson's wife was shot and killed tonight."

Joanna sat, frozen, as if Vanessa's words wouldn't come true if she remained completely still.

"How?"

"We don't know yet. Apparently, someone walked up to the front door, she opened, and they shot her."

"Nate and the kids?"

"He wasn't home. When he came back from work, the door wasn't locked. He walked in and found her right there...kids were upstairs. Their aunt is taking care of them now."

"Damn." Joanna needed stronger words, and a strong drink, to start with, though there wasn't much of anything that could do the situation justice. This time, she didn't need an extra hint. Nate had been her colleague. He had found and helped the victim of a man she'd killed. Even though Short had let Grace down, she'd probably never stopped blaming Joanna for Edward Short's death.

Who else would have an agenda against her?

"Theo looked into Lester?"

To her surprise, she heard Theo's voice. "We don't want to jump to conclusions here, but yes, we did. If she pulled this off, we have no idea how. The public defender was afraid of her. She doesn't have visitors."

"Guards? Blackmail?"

"Joanna, we haven't found anything yet."

"Keep looking. There's got to be a connection. I'm going to give you a few names now. Make sure these people are safe. I don't care about the budget."

"I'll be sure to let the lieutenant know," he said dryly. "Besides, we have thought of them already. I promise you we're not taking any chances."

It was cold comfort. Her eyes were stinging. She wasn't sure how much longer she could handle the emotional roller coaster.

But nothing could compare to the pain Nate had to feel. Joanna knew, because she'd almost been there.

"Okay. Thank you for letting me know."

"I wish we didn't have to," he said. "I want you two to be careful. It's all a little too much to be coincidence."

"I agree. One more thing. Could you send me the facial composite of the guy who beat up Lawrence?"

"I really shouldn't."

"Please. I'm not sure it will help, but if I can't think of anything, I'll just delete it."

He sighed. "I'll send it over when I get the chance."

"You have no doubt, right? That the two incidents are related?"

Joanna wished she didn't already know the answer.

"No. I'm sorry."

"Me too. Let me know when you catch that son of a bitch."

"I will," he promised. "And congratulations. I know this is a setback, but I'm happy for you. You deserve something good."

"Don't we all?" she wondered out loud, clicking end call. Rue wordlessly embraced her.

⁂

She'd allowed herself a weak moment. It couldn't last too long, or, Joanna feared, she'd never come back from it. She had washed her face and made the rounds of the house, making sure it was secure for the night. That helped some.

"I'm really sorry," Rue said when she came to bed.

"I'm sorry about earlier." Joanna felt fairly embarrassed about losing it the way she had. "I never even met her."

"You liked him."

"Yeah. Nate's a good guy. He doesn't deserve any of this shit." She drew a shuddering breath. "Well, neither do we, but here we are."

"Perhaps we could postpone the wedding plans for a bit," Rue suggested. "Who knows, they might solve the case quicker than we think. Maybe Theo and Vanessa would even like to come?"

"Let's not jinx it." Joanna laughed wryly. "Every time Vanessa calls it's something worse. I don't want to know what would have to happen to bring them here. But maybe we shouldn't wait." What she didn't say was—anything could happen. She didn't want to take any chances.

Chapter Fourteen

A couple of days passed by, then four, five, a week. No news, good or bad, from Vanessa and Theo. Given the past couple of times they'd spoken, Joanna considered it good news. Regardless, she couldn't get Nate and his family out of her mind. She'd thought about telling Theo to give Nate her condolences but decided against it. Chances were, he didn't want to be reminded of her, now, or ever, because she was connected to Danvers. There wasn't a doubt in her mind that the murder of his wife was related to the Short case, Danvers being the victim that got away, Joanna being the one who ended the killer.

She and Rue were going about their work at the inn, trying to keep the world outside of the island at bay best they could. They even succeeded for moments at a time—until Theo's message arrived.

Sorry for the delay, but we were really busy here. This is the description your father gave.

Joanna opened the file and nearly dropped her phone. She sat down in the chair in the waiting area for Denise's visitors and stared at the picture. This wasn't good.

The description Lawrence had given of his attacker fit a man she'd seen only recently, to a "t", the strange guest named Liam Preston. She tried to think of everything he'd said to her, everything that other guests had said about him. He'd hooked up with various people during his stay, according to Oliver.

Joanna got to her feet and knocked on the door of Denise's office, somewhat relieved to find Rue with her.

"We need to talk," she said.

"That doesn't sound good," Denise remarked. "I am right to assume it's not about wedding preparations?"

Joanna held the phone out to her.

"That looks suspiciously like…"

"Liam Preston. The asshole came here on vacation."

Rue looked shocked but didn't say anything.

"You're thinking this is more than a strange coincidence?"

"I'm afraid it is. The wife of a former colleague was murdered in her home. I think it's him. He came here because of me…and he has to know things."

Rue still hadn't said anything, listening to the conversation quiet and pale.

"Damn," Denise said. "This isn't good. We'll have to think of alternatives."

"What does that mean?" Rue wanted to know. "You're not going to kick us out?"

"Of course not, but we'll have to consider if it's still safe for you here. If he knew about Joanna, her father, that colleague…We don't know who else is in danger."

"I agree," Joanna said. "I came here first, but I need to talk to Theo. He'll look into it."

"You do that and lay low for the rest of the day. I can give Rue some time off. Talk to him and get back to me later?"

"Sure, thank you. Could you please check if the women who arrived on the same day are still here?"

"I'll do that but remember: Lay low."

Joanna nodded and turned to leave. Rue followed her silently.

"It will never end, right?" she asked, when she and Joanna were alone. "There is nowhere safe."

"There will be. I promise. Let's just get in the car, and I'll make the call."

⁓

"White male, mid-thirties maybe. He spent nine days here, hooked up with various people, most of which are gone by now. He was coming on to me on his first day but given his later activities I just figured he got over it."

Rue gave her a sharp look. They hadn't talked about Preston in detail. Joanna didn't think it was important at the time, now she wished she'd paid more attention. On the other hand, her, paying attention, might have been what got her on this man's radar. She thought of the guests watching from behind windows when the police picked up Harry Farrell. The sharply increased number of bookings after the murder.

"I'll check for any connections to Grace," Theo said. "Thank you. I would have gotten back to you earlier, but what are the odds?" He sounded resigned, as if he should have known the answer. Even in paradise, Joanna attracted trouble. She couldn't run from it, could she?

"Do it fast. There's no saying what he's going to do next." She sensed his hesitation, alarm bells going off in her mind. "Has there been another incident?" What a lousy understated way to say a woman was dead.

"No, but thanks for the reminder," he said dryly.

"Your sarcasm is misplaced. The guy was right here, and apparently, he has information about me. That thing he said to my father? He's trying to get me implicated."

"Come on. You weren't anywhere near Nate Gibson's residence."

115

"No, but...It's not random. I can feel it."

"We're doing everything we can," he promised.

"What about Allison? Does she still think I went off the deep end?"

"I'm gently steering her away from that theory."

"Good, and thank you for that. I wish I could help more."

"Yeah. It is what it is," he said cryptically.

"Anyone else still looking for me? Because of Short?"

"Are you kidding? We are busy looking for murderers."

After they ended the call, Joanna couldn't help the feeling that he'd sounded uneasy.

Marian Rickers composed herself quickly. Theo had seen the conflicting emotions in her expression, surprise, fear, curiosity. He hadn't seen her since the day he'd come to ask her if she'd, by any chance, heard from his partner Joanna Mitchell. That was before Joanna was arrested and convicted for the execution of a murderer. One of the man's victims had been Faith Rickers, Marian's niece.

"Detective. I haven't seen you in a long time. Come on in." In fact, he was fairly surprised she still recognized him. Then again, he and Joanna had visited her a few times under the most horrific circumstances.

"How have you been?" he asked, never a light question in his line of work.

She shrugged. "You can see. Still here."

Marian and Faith had been close. Before anything, Theo needed to test the waters as to how she felt about Joanna's actions. He hoped that they could go from there.

"I'm really sorry, about everything."

"I can imagine. It became quite the spectacle. Somewhere in there, I think too many people forgot about what happened to these young women."

He suppressed a wince. This wasn't going great.

"Would you like something to drink?" she asked. "I just made coffee."

"A coffee would be great, thank you."

She guided him to the living room and left for the adjacent kitchen, returning with two mugs a moment later.

"The other detective, Mitchell...? I thought about visiting her in prison," she said. "Then I didn't because I didn't want to run into any reporters. I guess she didn't expect things to turn out this way."

"No. She just wanted to make it stop."

"And she did, just not soon enough. For Faith, I mean. Then again, it was what any family member wished they could have done. I don't know if I'm grateful, but I'm not sorry. I can't imagine she is."

That was territory Theo didn't want to venture into, but perhaps he wasn't in a position as bad as he'd worried.

"Ms. Rickers, I came here, because...I was hoping you could put me in touch with a friend of yours. In fact, that could help Joanna a great deal."

He hadn't lied to Joanna when he said they were busy, still, this bore a risk. He was putting her future into a grieving woman's hands.

It might work out.

It had to.

Marian Rickers gave him a wry smile. "I see. You didn't come here after all these years to check up on me."

"I wanted to do that too. But yes, to be honest, I'm trying to help someone who has a lot on the line."

"Is she in trouble?"

"I think someone is trying to set her up, and it would be helpful if she could defend herself."

"I see. You want to wait and see if they put me through to the governor right away?"

"That would be great, thank you."

⁂

"I haven't seen you around much. What time are you off work?"

"...cocktail for you."

"That sounds great."

"I hope you enjoyed your stay."

"Like you wouldn't imagine."

Allison Kato listened to the recording once more, Joanna Mitchell talking to a man about cocktails and his stay at wherever she was. Part of Joanna's first sentence was cut off by white noise, but the rest of the conversation came across quite clearly. It sounded polite, friendly even, to her.

She cast a look at where Theo was sitting at his desk, on the phone. He had completely rejected her theory about Joanna being so angry at her father that she felt like she needed to send him a message. Now this recording. What was the truth? And why had her partner spent all morning on mysterious errands?

"Hey, Theo," she called, when she saw he was off the phone, and waved him over. "Come listen to this."

He was remarkably unimpressed regarding the obvious connection.

"Let's see if we can trace it? And get that recording out in case anyone recognizes the voice."

"Joanna's voice is in it too."

"Yeah, so? That guy was a guest at the hotel. They were bound to have some interactions."

"The hotel? So, I was right, you knew all along where she was? Theo, damn it!"

"What is your problem? We have a murder to solve, and we both know that Joanna didn't kill that woman. That guy, for some reason, has it in it for her. That's why he said what he said to Mitchell. We find him, this is over."

"It's not going to be that easy."

"Why not?"

"Don't be ridiculous. We'll need her here to testify."

"That's not likely to happen, and I don't see why we can't avoid it."

Allison shook her head. "I know you're all on some guilt trip about how you had to keep quiet the last time, and you felt you let her down. I can't cut her that much slack, and how do you know that she didn't crack under pressure, got involved with the wrong people?"

"Because she's planning her wedding! Look," he lowered his voice, "I'm aware of what's at stake here. I'd like to have her back here as well, check some boxes, but as you can imagine, it's complicated. We need to find that Preston guy before anything else."

"How do you imagine you can keep all of this under wraps?"

"I managed so far, didn't I?"

She held up her cell phone. "Let's just hope he doesn't send any more 'presents.'"

⟨⟩

Grace Lester hadn't exaggerated when she said that she had more than enough entertainment. Every once in a while, though, she wondered about the detective's visit. Joanna's complicated relationship with her father had been part of Grace's research at some point, but it was never an aspect she'd been especially interested in.

If she wanted to hurt Joanna, she wouldn't start with Lawrence Mitchell—or the Gibson family. Grace had heard talk about the murder, and she, too, was now intrigued as to who wanted to lure Joanna out.

So much that she got distracted.

When the door to her cell opened, the younger woman jumped to her feet, covering herself quickly. The guard didn't blink.

"Lester, you're coming with me."

"Where are we going?" She hadn't seen him before. He was attractive, but she had no trouble identifying the hint of cruelty in his smile. In her time in prison, Grace had quickly figured out that a lot of people could be played. She wasn't sure if that was a possibility with this one, and it bothered her.

"You'll see," he said curtly, and shackled her wrists on front of her. "Let's go, I don't have all day."

In her mind, Grace went through all the people she might have pissed off. Violet Short might put some blame on her for Edward's death, but she didn't have the means to pull this off. The victims' families...no.

Joanna?

She shook her head. This wasn't possible. Joanna wouldn't come after her for Rue, after all this time. She watched in awe as he led her through various doors, showing papers, no one stopping them. He pushed her into the back of a van, locked the doors and got in the front.

Grace was worried. She and Edward always made sure to choose their victims carefully, no rich college kids whose parents might want to start a vendetta, get shadowy people and dark money involved. A boyfriend?

She'd deny everything and make him believe that the murders, the choice of victim and the execution, had all been Edward's idea. There was nothing she could have done to help. She was a victim, just like them. As she continued to create her version of reality, she became calmer, certain she would get herself out of this bizarre situation.

When the van stopped not much later, she waited with a hammering heart for his return.

The double doors opened, and he climbed in with her.

"Who are you?"

"Your new best friend," he said and reached out to unlock her cuffs. "Now you owe me."

Chapter Fifteen

"**D**amn it! Tell me how the fuck could this happen!"

The warden was unimpressed in the face of Theo's rage. Puzzled, perhaps, but not as shocked as one might think, given the circumstances.

"We have a protocol in place. That's why we called you. As for how it happened, the son of a bitch came prepared. Had the uniform, the ID, papers...everything he needed to walk right out with her."

"And you're telling me there was no previous contact whatsoever?"

They were looking for a man named Liam Preston, though it was doubtful this was his real name. There was no connection. To Joanna. To Grace.

Together with Allison, Theo had spent hours trying to figure out the mystery. Now, of course, their problems had become much bigger. They had a serial killer on the run helped by someone they assumed to be a murderer as well. Grace was staying true to her M.O., having a man by her side again.

There was no mistaking their goal: To kill.

Days like these, he was tired of the job.

He still had to warn Joanna, but first, he had to put plan B into motion.

After he got his phone back from the locker, Theo called Marian Rickers.

"I'm sorry to bother you again," he said. "It's urgent. I need some reassurances."

"I'll get back to you as soon as I can," she promised.

He scrolled back to the picture of Liam Preston, wondering again why he had taken it upon himself to get Grace out.

"Who the hell are you?" he said out loud.

⁂

Joanna wished she could spend her days in blissful ignorance, just for one moment, but apparently it wasn't meant for her. Perhaps Tamara's and Alexandra's respective stories hadn't ended in tragedy.

But Nate? She felt guilty even though it was irrational. Whoever felt like they had to even a score with her was using innocent people as pawns.

It had to stop. She needed to make it stop.

Rue turned to her, hiding a yawn behind her hand.

"We're not going to sleep, are we?"

"Doesn't look that way."

2:18 a.m.

Joanna sat up against the headboard, shivering even though the night was mild as always.

"We might not be able to stay here." There was no point in trying to avoid the inevitable.

"I guess we've established by now that I'll go anywhere you go."

"This would be different. We'd be even more off the radar. We couldn't talk to anyone."

"You're suggesting running away from home? And our jobs? What about food?" Rue's tone was still light, a bit amused even, as if she didn't believe Joanna was serious. Was she?

Would this help anyone? She didn't know anymore.

"I'll never let you go hungry."

"I'll hold you to that, and you could start right now. Since we're not sleeping, let's get up and make a snack, okay?"

They went into the kitchen where Rue opened the door of the fridge and took out some fruit and cheese. Joanna stood in the middle of the room, not at all sure where to go from here as she watched Rue get more food out of the pantry.

Finally, Rue turned to her and embraced her tightly.

"None of this is your fault," she said. "Get it out of your head."

"They would have never come after Nate's wife if it wasn't for me—"

"Stop it. Now."

Joanna finally halted her thoughts enough to take a deep breath.

"I'm alive because of you. That's what you should be thinking."

You could say the same about me, Joanna thought, but she didn't say it out loud.

⁕

The hits kept on coming, Theo thought as he and Allison watched the security footage from the prison. At this point, they weren't surprised that the man who got Grace Lester out was Liam Preston, clad in the uniform, arriving with all the right papers. The questions remained. How? Most of all—why?

Theo had a few theories going back to his time when he and Joanna talked about the slasher daily. Bizarre as it was, murderers gained notoriety and admirers. It wasn't too far-fetched to think that Preston felt "inspired" by Grace's story? Theo wished he could still bounce off theories with Joanna in a professional setting, selfish as that might be.

He hadn't supported her during what had to have been the most difficult time of her life. None of them had because Vanessa and the department's leaders had made it very clear what the party line was: They didn't condone vendetta, not because anyone felt sorry for Decker. The next killer could get off on a technicality because a cop threw out the book. Another cop might get away with something less righteous. Slippery slope and all. It seemed to make sense back then, but he wondered if those words still had meaning. If things could have been different, had he been a better friend to Joanna back then.

But Joanna's life wasn't bad, with a home and a job on the island, the beach only a few minutes' drive away...with Rue.

Perhaps he was paranoid, having set something unnecessary into motion, but Theo felt relieved to know that this time, they had the powers that be on their side. Ironic to think that part of the governor's platform was strong opposition to the death penalty.

Confronted with a monster like Decker, or Short, principles wavered. Right or wrong? At this point, all he wanted was to get Lester and Preston behind bars. Perhaps there was something they could do afterwards to ensure the legal status and safety for Joanna and Rue, give them more options—and Vanessa might like to spend a few days on the island too. They'd have a chance for overdue conversations.

"Are you dreaming?" Allison chastised him. "This is not good."

"No, it's not, but hopefully we'll have the chance to catch those two jailbirds with one stone."

She chuckled. "I'm not sure how I feel about your metaphors, but damn, I hope we get a break in this case soon. How is Joanna by the way?"

His first impulse was to divert. They had an urgent job to do after all. Theo didn't give in to it. They needed all the allies they could get, and Allison was one in spite of the fact she'd had the wrong idea about Joanna and her father.

"She's good," he said. "Let's hope it stays that way."

"Detectives…" The young officer peeking inside the room looked apologetic. "A couple of tourists found a body in the park."

"We'll be right there." Theo turned to the tech who had shown them the video. "Thank you. We'll be back."

❦

Allison Kato winced as she crouched down beside the body in the taped off area. The victim was sitting up against a tree. They were mostly sheltered by tall bushes, something for which she was grateful.

Trying to take in every possible clue, she pushed back against the anger that was flaring in her mind, creating an uncomfortable heat. Only for a split-second, Allison wondered what it would be like to give in to that anger the moment she had the perpetrator in front of her. It wasn't right. None of this should ever be about her, and all about the victim. Dignity. Justice. Not the headlines.

Truth be told, part of her still envied Joanna for tossing all of that aside, deciding that somebody who did this to another human being shouldn't be alive.

The woman was dressed for a night out, in a sleeveless short dress, wearing bracelets and a necklace. No shoes. Her purse was in her lap.

With gloved hands, Allison opened the clutch, producing a small wallet complete with ID, credit cards, loyalty cards for various stores and five twenty-dollar bills.

"Not a robbery then," Theo said behind her, the same anger belying the sarcasm he was trying to convey. Cynical they all were. Some days it was harder to keep up appearances.

"Maggie Simmons, twenty-seven," she read from the driver's license. "All the information is right there. They wanted us to have it."

"They? We are really already thinking that?"

"How many people do we suspect are on a killing spree right now?"

He flinched. Allison didn't blame him. It was a horrific thought either way.

She could not longer avoid looking at the woman, Maggie, whose eyes were wide open, seemingly staring at a horror only she could see. Her face was smudged with dirt and blood, streaked with tears.

What was the right punishment for someone who had done this? And a woman who had helped him? Death seemed like an option, though it was too quick, too easy. An eye for an eye? She couldn't afford to think this, ever, at a crime scene.

But Joanna hadn't always envisioned taking out murderers. How long had she resisted?

"You have a point." He looked around. "They didn't kill her here, too much potential exposure."

"You think Grace's M.O. is still the same?"

She and her former boyfriend had chosen their victims together and then seduced them for what was supposedly a consensual threesome, until it turned to murder. Lester and Short had operated like that for years, but Preston was still an unknown figure.

Allison turned the purse around, realizing her gloves were sticky with blood. She turned her attention back to the body, the flimsy dress. For the first time in years, Allison Kato had to fight back the urge to throw up at a crime scene. The fabric wasn't the color she'd first thought it was.

Trying to calm her breathing, she took another look at the woman's wallet. Behind the many cards, she found a photograph that had been folded in two to fit the pocket.

Allison opened it to reveal a picture of Joanna shaking Liam Preston's hand.

For a second or two, she and Theo stood speechless, because there wasn't a swear word strong enough for any of it.

"I need to tell you something," he said. "You can't share this with anyone."

Chapter Sixteen

In the early morning hours, Joanna had accepted the fact that she wouldn't be able to go back to sleep, too much running through her mind. Did history have to repeat itself, with no chance of ever changing the story? Or was it just her?

She had made coffee and taken a cup out on the deck, but the sights around her failed to calm her. Rue had asked valid questions. Where could they go from here?

There were no safe spaces—or perhaps it was all Joanna's fault, always had been, because she couldn't leave things alone. She could have taken down Decker with the help of a SWAT team, instead of going after him with the intent to execute him. Same with Short?

As Joanna sipped her coffee, she came to the same conclusion she had before. She would have likely done the same thing then, and now, when she couldn't turn away from Alexandra's distress, even at personal costs. She hated to admit it but perhaps Grace had had a point when she insisted they were both hunters.

The difference? Grace had chosen to, and experienced pleasure from causing others pain. All Joanna wanted was for it to stop. She'd come to a point where she'd learned that it was as much about her own pain as it was for the victims' justice. She wasn't completely unselfish. That didn't mean she was completely wrong, was it?

Something was in the air. Another change. Joanna could feel it. It wasn't much of a stretch to think that Grace wanted her to suffer. This new guy had an agenda, and it seemed that he wanted to please Grace. They wouldn't let her be. At the same time, Joanna would have to face the consequences of her actions.

The most important thing in all of this was that Rue would still be safe.

The subject of her thoughts came to quietly join her, her own coffee in hand. Barefoot in her shorts and tank top, her hair still tousled from sleep, Rue was so beautiful it hurt Joanna to look at her. Because she had to do what was right for her, and maybe she had fooled herself thinking it meant they could be together. Maybe not. She was tired.

"Come here," she said. Rue put her cup on the table and sat on her lap. Joanna pulled her close, resting her head against Rue's chest.

"It's different this time," Rue said, stroking her hair. "You are not alone in this anymore."

She had barely finished the sentence when they heard the sound of the helicopter.

⁂

Joanna's fears were confirmed sooner than she had imagined when a visitor knocked on their door. Joanna could tell that Rue hadn't made the connection yet. She didn't seem alarmed.

"I'll get it." Joanna got to her feet, her heart hammering as she went to the front door and opened it. Theo looked uncomfortable in his suit and tie, too hot for the climate, or because he had unpleasant news to share? She assumed it could be both.

"I thought you might come at some point. You didn't bring cuffs, so that's something."

Her joke came out as bland as she'd feared, and she could tell he didn't appreciate it much. "But I'm aware you didn't come here on a vacation either. Let's make this quick and painless."

"Grace Lester escaped," he said. "And they already killed together. I'm afraid this changes a lot."

"I assume," she said, stepping back though her mind was frozen in shock, part of her surprised she'd been able to move and talk. This couldn't be. How could she get out? Joanna gave herself the answer. Her new boyfriend had done for her what Edward Short wouldn't, lay it all on the line to free her. "Can I get you anything? We were just making breakfast. What do you need from me?"

"That's a good question, isn't it?" Rue asked when they walked into the kitchen. "Why would you think Joanna could help you with any of this?"

Joanna could tell from Theo's expression that he hadn't missed the suspicious tone.

"I swear, I will explain everything to you. Breakfast would be great, to be honest. I haven't had much time."

Rue sighed and took out a cup and plate for him. After adding a knife, fork and spoon, she closed the utensils drawer with more force than necessary.

They sat down. Joanna started to eat, assuming that not long from now, she wouldn't have an appetite any longer. She could feel Rue's gaze on her.

"I know it has to be bad. Otherwise, you wouldn't be here," she finally said.

"When you helped the women earlier..."

"I'm not going to apologize for that. Rue and I would know better than to look away."

"I'm not asking you to apologize. It was only a blip on the radar. We contained it, it would have been fine. This is different. It's possible that when Preston came here, he already knew about you, and if that's true...He likely had a plan that included your father and Nate Gibson's wife."

"And, apparently, breaking Grace out of prison."

Talking about the woman never failed to make her sick. Their hook-up at a time when desperate times had seemed to call for even more desperate measures would haunt her forever, regardless of the fact that she hadn't known who, what, Grace Lester was.

"They started out trying to frame you, but now they're already following their own ritual. It's something that points to them rather than to you. I wonder why."

"Because they can't help themselves?" Rue suggested, her tone dripping with sarcasm.

"Oh, they can," Joanna said grimly. "They just choose not to. Whatever their plan is with me, instant gratification is more important to them. Who is the victim?"

Truth be told, it wasn't the first thing she'd wanted to ask. Theo still hadn't given away the reason for his impromptu visit.

"A woman, late twenties, was last seen in a club talking to a good-looking guy."

"They can't be this fast without a lot of planning. Appearance, a place to stay. He studied Short and Lester's M.O. before he set the plan in motion. He has to have some money too."

She didn't like that Theo looked guilty at that.

"All right, as much fun as this is—no, I'm not serious, but it's a fact that I'm not on the department's payroll. Before I share any more of my valuable insights, I want the truth. Why are you really here?"

Rue sat up straighter.

Theo picked up his cup, drank a sip, and set it down.

"I need you to come with me."

Her stomach lurched, even though this wasn't a huge surprise for Joanna. No cuffs, that was merely decorum.

"How is this going to work?"

"No," Rue said, startling them both. "That's not the question here at all. Can he make us go?"

The lines were drawn. Joanna looked at Theo, waiting for an answer—to both questions.

"Rue, I can't make you do anything," he said as he took a folder out of the bag he'd brought. "Joanna...that's more complicated, but I think I found a solution that's going to work for all of us."

"Let's hear it."

"I'll go with the bad news first."

Rue scoffed. Joanna shook her head.

"The escaped serial murderer who's on the prowl again, wasn't the bad news? Jesus."

He took a copy out of the folder and laid it onto the table. "In addition to this, we have an audio recording, a conversation you had with Preston. It might be manipulated. In any case, they forced our hand, and we needed to get ahead of all of this. You remember Marian Rickers."

"Faith's aunt," Joanna said immediately.

"You know we need to do all of this by the book, so when we find them, we can make sure none of them will ever see the light of day. Thanks to Marian, I was able to talk to Governor O'Neal and explain our situation."

"What does that mean?" Rue's suspicion had given way to confusion.

"Joanna, I promise you it's safe for you to come with me. We need all the information we can get on this guy, and Grace, anything you can think of. Logistically, it just makes more sense for you to be there. We have your back. The governor is on our side."

Something still didn't add up. Joanna didn't think it was time for relief yet.

"A quid pro quo? I help you with the case, and if that works out, everyone will continue to look the other way?"

Theo didn't deny the truth of her statement.

"You have nothing to fear. I swear."

"We can't just talk here, and you make a note in your report? If the governor is on our side, can't she take my word for it? You know everything I know about Lester. Preston was hitting on me, to get a picture and some audio, or he meant it, I don't know. He had several hookups while he was here. That's all I know."

"Perhaps more will come to you. I could have you take a look at the evidence."

"I don't want that. In fact, I don't want anything to do with this, but I can understand you had some questions. I answered them best I could."

"Joanna." Theo sighed. "Governor O'Neal wants to see you."

"Why?" The question came from Joanna and Rue in perfect unison.

"I don't know, closure? Isn't that something we could all use? You can come back here and live happily ever after, and no one's ever going to bother you, ever again."

"That's motivating." Rue mumbled. "When do we have to go?"

"I'm not sure you should. I don't want you anywhere near her."

"Well, you won't have a choice, because I'm not staying here by myself."

Theo looked from her to Joanna, the semblance of a smile on his face.

"You have until noon to pack. We'll take the chopper, and the plane leaves at 2:15."

Joanna had the sudden urge to lean forward and put her head between her knees, lightheaded at the idea that tonight, they could be back in the city, a place she never wanted to see again.

"I swear this isn't some sort of trap. It's the best we can do."

"You need something, someone to bait her."

"No, Joanna. You know that's not how it works. We don't put civilians at risk."

He looked embarrassed though, which told her she hadn't been too far off. To her surprise, Joanna realized the term civilian still struck her as strange, and he knew it, playing to her ego just a little bit. Or maybe he was telling the whole truth, desperate to get a couple of murderers off the streets.

"I'm not saying it won't work. My only condition is that Rue be safe, whatever she decides."

"Whatever I decide?" Rue echoed, sounding exasperated. "You are really going to do this?"

"Theo is asking nicely. I appreciate that. I don't think the next cop coming here will do that."

"This is fucking unfair."

Rue barely ever swore, but Joanna couldn't help thinking she had a point. Regardless.

"All those promises you made, you got them in writing?"

Theo nodded. "I thought you'd never ask."

⚬

In the privacy of their bedroom, Rue didn't resist when Joanna embraced her from behind.

"We knew this day might come."

"Sure," Rue acknowledged. "I just wonder what it was all for, Vanessa pulling all those strings to get us here. If it's safe for you to be back there, why didn't they say so? What changed?" What if nothing had changed and Joanna would be arrested the moment they went through customs? "I think we could still run. I don't even care about a house or jobs any longer."

"You heard Theo. There's no need to run. And he could be right. I helped them with Grace the first time."

"For Christ's sake, that shouldn't be your job. They have actual cops for that, people who, as you pointed out earlier, get paid."

"I know, but..." Joanna sounded pensive. "Maybe this is a chance we can't afford to miss."

"We already had that chance," Rue pointed out. "We have a life here, work...Remember how unhappy you were when you found out I was working for your dad? I can finally breathe. We go back, it's where it all happened. How can this be good for anything?"

"I'll have to see what Governor O'Neal has to say. We'll go from there."

Abruptly, Rue stepped out of the embrace. "I'll be back, but I need to talk to someone first."

"I understand. I'll let Denise know, and we'll come back here to pack?"

Rue blinked back tears. "I guess that's what we'll do."

Chapter Seventeen

Zach didn't seem surprised when Rue told him she wouldn't come back for some time.

"I heard you guys had a visitor."

"News travels fast," she acknowledged. He sat next to her on a bench.

"Listen, I haven't known you for long, and you've made amazing progress. You'll be okay."

Rue gave him a faint smile. "I appreciate you saying that."

"I'm not just saying that. You went at the bad guy during your therapy session. I think you can handle pretty much anything that comes your way."

"He was an average criminal. What we're dealing with now is pure evil."

"You need some spiritual guidance?"

"No," she said right away. "I need them to leave us alone."

"Be careful," he advised. "Don't take on more than your share."

"That's okay." Rue got to her feet. "I'm just starting to take on my share. Thank you for everything."

"You did all the hard work. Take care, Rue." The solemn exchange made it clear they both knew this might be the last time they saw each other. She was fine with the firm hug that would have made her jump out of her skin when she first arrived on the island.

She would do her share.

Twenty-four hours ago, they hadn't even known they'd have to leave. Now they were on a plane bringing them back to the place that harbored all of Joanna's demons, still. The father who had rejected her. A serial killer, and then another, that had taunted her. The voice she'd almost silenced on the island, whispering to her that it was all her fault. She had no time for any of this. Look at the evidence, share her thoughts, speak to the governor.

Joanna had to admit she was curious about this arrangement. She had met Marian Rickers when she and Theo worked the slasher case, had been vaguely aware of her association with the governor, but that was it.

She studied Theo's body language when they got into the customs line. He didn't expect any bad surprises. Joanna's stomach was in knots, and she could feel the tension radiating off of Rue's body.

The agent looked at her, her picture, and asked the standard questions.

"It's for work. We'll be visiting friends too. I expect to be back in a couple of weeks," she said. He stamped her passport and handed it back to her. Just like that.

Rue followed, and then they were on the other side.

"I feel hurt," Theo said. "Neither one of you believed me."

"To be honest, I don't know what to believe anymore, but I want Grace back behind bars just as much," Joanna told him.

"Good. I'll bring you to the hotel, and I'll get you in the morning so you can make your official statement."

"Sounds like a plan."

On another occasion, Joanna would have loved to be in this place with Rue. Someone had spared no expenses to make their stay comfortable. She was convinced it couldn't be the department.

They rode up the elevator to the fifteenth floor.

"It's at the end of the hall," Theo explained.

Joanna stiffened when she saw the woman standing next to the door, easily identified by her stance as a plain clothes law enforcement officer.

"Breathe. You told me I had to make sure Rue was safe, and besides, you're a valuable witness. We don't want to take any chances."

Theo nodded to the officer, opened the door to the room and handed Joanna the key card.

"Don't raid the minibar."

Joanna stepped inside and found herself being enveloped into a tight hug the next moment.

"Oh, that's right," Theo said. "I thought we could all have dinner tonight."

Vanessa stepped back, smiling. "I hate the circumstances, I really do, but it's good to see you both. You look amazing, but I guess that's what being lazy on the beach for months does to a person."

"That, and catching a few criminals."

"Yeah, we'll get to that part later. I'll leave you alone for now. Dinner at seven?"

"Sounds good."

They weren't in this alone. With the support of Theo, Vanessa, and an influential politician, would the story change this time?

Rue was dangerously close again to feeling like she was going out of her skin. She was also irrationally angry at Joanna who acted like they were on a vacation, meeting up with a couple of old friends. She was aware that Theo and Vanessa had risked a great deal for both of them, and grateful for it, though she didn't think she and Joanna owed them that much.

Vanessa had been making up for the fact that she'd helped put Joanna in prison all those years ago. Theo, her former partner, had taken a long time to come around.

As far as Rue was concerned, they were even. Friendly, polite, but even.

"Grace thinks that these men are impressed with her, but she's fooling herself," she said. "Short said she wanted a ritual because she thought that was something real serial killers had to have. He mocked her for that."

It didn't seem like appropriate dinner conversation, but as soon as the thought came to her mind, she couldn't hold it back.

Both Theo and Joanna stared at her in alarm.

"What? It's what he said to me. He wanted to record himself killing me and get the footage to her somehow. I don't think it was to share. He wanted to brag, show her what he could do while she was stuck in prison."

"Rue," Theo said softly. "None of this was in your statement. You could barely remember anything."

"Nothing much has changed. It's still a haze for the most part..." She didn't finish her sentence, trying to grasp what had just happened. "But he said those things. I remember them." Rue wasn't sure whether that was a good thing, even though Dr. Shepherd had told her that some memories might come back to her, and when they did, they would work on containing them.

"Grace was in over her head, though she'd never admit it," Joanna said. She kept her voice low, for whose benefit, Rue wasn't sure. It didn't make the subject matter any less gruesome. "My guess is she found another guy, and soon enough he'll try to make her take the fall for him. But I don't want to discuss this now. There have to be some boundaries."

"I agree," Vanessa said with a quick look to Rue. "First things first. Tomorrow, we'll work at the station."

"Didn't you say you left Internal Affairs?" Rue asked her.

"Yes."

"So how did that go?" She wasn't making polite small talk. She wanted to know for sure if Vanessa had any power to protect them.

"Well," Vanessa returned. "I'm in the private sector now, but I still consult with the department from time to time."

Rue wasn't sure whether she'd gotten an answer to her question at all.

⚭

Joanna hadn't always been good at making the best out of a bad situation. She figured that this time, the best they could hope for was to stay under the radar until they could go back home. She was going to give her official statement. No one was going to arrest her. Grace couldn't know that she and Rue were here. Everything was good, wasn't it?

"You've been ignoring me for her. That was always a mistake," Grace whispered as she ran the cold blade across Joanna's exposed skin, taunting her. She wasn't afraid of her, not of pain, or death. What was making her sick to her stomach was that she once had willingly let the woman touch her. There was no excuse, no escape from that.

Joanna shrank away when Grace turned the knife in her hand, the sharp side of the blade making contact, breaking skin.

"I said I was sorry. Why do you want to hurt me?" She couldn't move or raise her voice below a whisper.

"Because I get you. Because you want me to," Grace said and pushed the knife into her stomach right where a line had been drawn with a black marker. Joanna's own scream woke her up.

"Joanna? It's okay. Please come back to me."

Rue's voice was calm and warm, slowly drawing her back into reality and her safe surroundings. There was no knife, no blood—no Grace.

Joanna drew a shaky breath.

"That was a bad one. I'm so sorry." Rue reached out tentatively, touching her shoulder. "Not for the nightmare, that wasn't me, obviously. But for being a bitch all evening. Come here."

"You weren't. Not even close." She let herself be drawn into an embrace, Rue's heartbeat against her ear helping to calm her own.

Joanna cursed the days when she'd thought nothing of sleeping with a woman she'd met the same night. Ironic that Rue might not be here with her if she hadn't suspended her "no one-night stands" rule.

"I hate giving her this much space in my brain," she admitted. "Maybe Theo was right. If I can help catch her...That might make things better for all of us."

"I'm with you, whatever you need," Rue murmured. "Just don't take on more than your share."

After Joanna and Rue had breakfast from the hotel's buffet, Theo came to get them. Just Joanna, in theory, but everyone had accepted that she wasn't going anywhere without Rue.

She wasn't sure what kind of greeting she'd expected, but at the station, everyone was going about their work. No one paid much attention to them when they walked to the conference room Theo had reserved for this purpose.

His partner Allison Kato was already there. She got up to greet both Joanna and Rue.

"I'm glad you could both be here," she said, her expression guarded. "We have coffee, tea, water, and pastries." Allison gestured to a side table behind her. "Just help yourself if you'd like anything."

"That's all right. We already had breakfast," Joanna said.

"Great. Then we can get started." Allison cast a pensive look at Rue. "I'm generally not opposed to the idea of you being here, but there's something I'd like to talk to Joanna about alone. If we could get this out of the way first?"

The hesitation and dread were almost comical, Joanna thought. Separation anxiety. They'd managed eventually, on the island, but here, neither of them had a reason to be too trusting, or careless.

"I'll wait outside," Rue said. "It's a police station. Nothing bad can happen to me here, can it?"

"I'll wait with you," Theo offered, and they left the room while Allison and Joanna sat down across from each other.

❧

"You're sure you don't need anything?" Theo asked.

Rue shook her head. "Like Joanna said, we had breakfast, and this isn't going to take long. I might have another coffee later."

"Sure."

They spent a few awkward minutes in silence. Rue noticed that most desks were empty. She assumed that Grace's escape required a lot of manpower. What a strange, antiquated word to use in this context, she thought. Cops, managers...women could be anything these days. Even serial killers. Language hadn't caught up fast enough. Or perhaps they were fooling themselves thinking that lasting change could be possible.

"What are you thinking?"

"I'm thinking about the word manpower," Rue told him, almost amused at the way he tried to hide his confusion. "Look, we don't have to pretend. Neither Joanna nor I would be here if we had the choice. We appreciate what you've been doing to protect us. Thank you. You don't have to make small talk or entertain me."

"Fair enough. I'll admit I'm glad you're here. Joanna was always good at this."

"Kato isn't?"

"She is, but she's not the one who's looking for redemption," he said. As if Rue needed a reminder.

⁂

Joanna didn't need any more proof. Allison Kato still didn't trust her, and perhaps she had reason to, after the night she'd run out on her, hell-bent on saving Rue.

"If you had any trouble because of me, I'm sorry," she offered.

"Don't worry about it. Trying to put Grace Lester and her boyfriend away is our highest priority. In fact, it's our only priority. But for that it's important we put all the pieces together correctly. Do you remember ever telling her about your father?"

The question puzzled Joanna. Was she still holding on to that theory?

"I don't think Grace was ever interested in him, and no, we didn't talk about him. He probably came up as part of her research. If Preston wanted her attention, he might have done the same research."

"When he stayed at the inn, you never talked about your father either?"

"No, of course not." Joanna was beginning to get irritated with her. "Where are you going with this? He was a guest. A bit creepy, but we still kept it polite. That's about it. There was no reason whatsoever to share anything personal with him."

"You had cocktails together?"

"What? Of course not."

Allison produced a tablet. "This was sent to me not long ago, just before Preston broke her out. Listen."

"Sure."

Joanna easily recognized her voice and Liam Preston's. "Yeah, Theo told me about this. It's definitely manipulated. I didn't know he recorded any of our conversations. He cut them together so it would look like we met for a drink."

"Why would he do that?"

"I don't know. He, or they, wanted to set me up, taunt me...It worked, didn't it? I'm here."

"Okay."

Joanna sensed there was more, so she opted for a pre-emptive strike.

"About that other theory of yours, you're wrong. I had no part in what happened to my father. We're not close as you know, but I didn't have any reason to hate him that much."

"All right, Joanna, thank you. I think we can bring Rue and Theo back in."

Chapter Eighteen

S he'd been right not to let down her guard too easily, Joanna reflected, when she later sat with Theo over the crime scene photos. Vanessa had come by and convinced Rue to go to the hotel with her. He might truly think she could help, and perhaps the governor felt the same, but Allison Kato was still wary. Joanna couldn't blame her after the brief history they'd had, and all the rumors she'd probably heard over the years.

She'd be wary of herself.

The truth remained the same. Grace and Preston were out there, probably preparing the next kill.

"How much do you know about the victim?"

"She was a second-year resident at Graham General. Friends told us she said she'd stay home and study that night, but apparently, she went to that bar instead."

"You think they chose her at random? Grace and Edward stalked their victims before they approached them."

"They didn't have a lot of time to do this, with Grace just out."

Joanna pondered his words, a thought springing to mind that made her jump to her feet.

"What is it? Jesus, give a guy a warning!"

"Christina Danvers. Do you know where she is?"

"I think she left town after she finished her therapy."

"She's a loose end. My dad, the Gibson family, this is all connected. You have to contact her, make sure she's okay. Damn, why didn't I think of this earlier?

Theo didn't argue. "I'll be right back," he said.

Joanna stood in the doorway where she saw him conferring with an officer. A couple of minutes later, he joined her again.

"Why would he want to help Grace tie up loose ends?"

"He's in love?"

"Where does he find her? Online? The dark web? People daring each other to break a dangerous criminal out of prison? He had official ID and forms!"

"Someone on the inside?" Joanna suggested. "They got him copies or software? I thought he was creepy, but he had a lot of action during his vacation. Psychopaths can be charming."

"We questioned the staff. Nothing came up."

"You can get me those transcripts?"

"With all due respect, we went over all of this multiple times..."

"You wanted me to come here," she reminded him, and he relented.

"I'll get them."

"What about facial recognition from that photo?"

"Not clear enough. We made portions of the tape available to the public—nothing."

"Okay. He might be using different accents. Denise gave you the credit card number, I assume? Nothing yet?"

"No hits. They were so damn blatant, dumping her body right there in the park. Something has to come up."

It will, Joanna thought. It's only a matter of time. But then, in the case of the slasher, it had taken eleven years. None of them could go through that again.

Grace stumbled and barely avoided stepping into a puddle of blood. Instead of the familiar high, she felt light-headed, almost sick. Was she getting soft?

No, she decided. Killing was an art form, or at least it had been to her and Edward. To Joanna, it was a self-righteous way of dealing with the world, and Grace still hoped she'd deal with her at some point. Not today or tomorrow. They had to get the hell out of here.

Liam, or Chuck, as he had told her to call him this week, didn't care much for art, or seduction. He was a butcher. She brushed her fingers over her cheek, startled to see the crimson on her fingertips.

He had made a fucking mess, now whistling in the shower.

Without thinking, she went inside the bathroom and opened the door to the stall.

"What the hell were you thinking? We don't have time!"

He regarded her with curiosity.

"You have nothing to say?"

Within a split-second, he grabbed her wrist so tightly she let out a pained yelp, and he dragged her close enough for some of the water to get on her hair and clothes. "If there's not much time, I suggest you start cleaning the hell up."

He let go of her so abruptly she nearly fell. Sure, he had gotten her out and bestowed a lot of flattery on her at first, but she was beginning to doubt the wisdom of her actions following her escape. He was soiling her legacy. No one was worth that. She could give the detectives some clues and have him arrested within the hour. Did he ever think of that?

When Grace saw the look he gave her, her anger vanished giving way to something she'd rarely experienced at Edward's side. Fear? She wasn't afraid of anyone.

"You can have the next one, babe," he said, something in his tone sending a shiver down her spine. "We'll do it your way."

"You bet your ass we will," she mumbled, but her unease remained.

❧

Joanna wasn't sure about Theo, but to her, the day was a success as they'd managed to determine that Christina Danvers was safe at her home. No one had approached her. She couldn't report anything out of the ordinary.

It didn't mean she wasn't on the killers' radar. It could mean someone else was.

She met Vanessa and Rue in the hotel bar where Vanessa shared the itinerary she and Theo had decided on.

"In the morning, you can go back to the station, see if anything comes up. Later in the evening, the governor will see you. In between...Well, I guess you have some free time. You could see someone if you like."

"Like who? I don't want to put anyone in danger. They might not know we're here, but it's probably not that hard to find out."

"As you wish. After you've spoken to Governor O'Neal...I don't see why Theo would want to keep you for much longer, frankly, but you don't have to be in a rush either."

"What if we are?" Rue asked. "There are friends waiting for us, a home, wedding preparations...I would like to see my parents though if that's possible."

"I'm sure we can arrange that." There had been a flash of hurt on Vanessa's face when Rue didn't include her in their group of friends, but she got over it quickly. "And Joanna?"

"What about me? Kira maybe."

Rue and Vanessa shared a look Joanna found curious. She made the connection.

"No, thanks. I don't think there's anything that would change the opinion we have of each other."

"It's more for you than for him," Rue said softly. "This might be the last time for real."

With a start, Joanna realized she might be right. She had wasted opportunities, and her regrets had little to do with Lawrence...but they were related.

"Yes, sure, I'll see him. I'm sure he was ready to believe I sent someone to beat him up."

"You can ask him," Rue said. "I can come with you."

"You know what he's going to say."

Vanessa's interested gaze said she wasn't completely following their conversation.

"Maybe for once, something will make a Goddamn difference to him," Rue said with surprising passion. "He could have died. We were all in danger. He could have a change of heart, give a tiny hint that he actually has one."

Joanna feared Rue would be disappointed, but she couldn't help hoping that Lawrence might have something for her, even if it wasn't forgiveness or acceptance.

"Okay then," she said. "While we're here, let's meet the parents."

❦

The last time Joanna had seen her father was shortly before Vanessa helped her disappear. She had threatened him, desperate to make sure he wouldn't interfere with Rue's career, because at that time, she didn't believe that she and Rue could have a future.

She didn't call him. Vanessa did, and she drove the two of them. Their security detail followed in an unmarked vehicle.

Lawrence Mitchell still lived in the same three-story house Joanna had grown up in, something close to a mansion. She was sure her old room had been turned into a storage or guest room, not that the house lacked space.

An employee opened the door to them with an impassive expression.

"Follow me, please."

She led them into the living area where Lawrence Mitchell stood with a woman not much older than Joanna. She smiled politely, reaching out a hand.

"Hi, I'm Renée Madison. We've been working, but I'll leave you to it now. Rue, good to see you again."

"You too, Renée."

"Your friend said you wanted to see me," Lawrence Mitchell said before he sat down on the couch, not offering them a seat.

Joanna sat on the couch across from him and after some hesitation, Rue took a seat next to her.

"Frankly," he continued, "I didn't expect to see either of you again, but I guess you're going to tell me why you're here any minute now."

"I heard what happened. I'm really sorry."

"That took you a while."

Rue winced, but this was nothing new to Joanna.

"I'm sorry about that too. How are you?" In the few months that had passed since their last meeting, he had aged. She had seen it before in victims of crime, especially someone like Lawrence who thought of himself as invincible. Come to think of it, they were similar that way. She had the streaks of gray to show for it.

"I'm fine as you can see. Don't tell me you're here to ask me that. And whatever it is you two are planning, I'm not going to attend a fake wedding, no matter how you want to dress it up."

"Don't worry Mr. Mitchell. We're not planning a fake wedding. It's called a wedding, and I think I speak for both of us when I say we only want people who care about us there."

Joanna wasn't sure if she should laugh or cry.

"Poor Rue," he said, shaking his head. "I can remember when you were a professional. You had a reputable life before my daughter. Well, she does that to people."

"Thanks, Dad. I can tell you're doing fine, so I won't bother you for much longer. Don't worry, Rue is right about the wedding. I'm not going to try to change your mind, but there is something you could help me with. Do you know where Mom is?"

She could tell from the shocked silence hitting her that neither Lawrence nor Rue had expected this question. Up until this moment, Joanna hadn't been sure she'd find the courage to ask it, but her father's attitude made it clear she didn't have any time to waste.

"Why would you ask that? You think she's going to give you away?"

"Dad, please."

"I'm not sure what you want to do with that information, anything that isn't foolish, that is—but yes, I know where she is. Or at least, where she was until last year, I'm not sure if that's still correct."

"Dear God." No longer depending on a paycheck from Lawrence Mitchell, Rue had few reservations to speak her mind. "Do you even understand how cruel this is?"

"It's easy to judge. Believe it or not, there was a time when I still had hope for what Joanna could be without her mother's influence. But like Joanna, she couldn't stay out of trouble. I guess it's right what they say about the apple and the tree. I kept an eye on her. I had to. Joanna might be wrong, but unlike her mother, she isn't weak."

Joanna didn't want this conversation to go on longer than absolutely necessary, not only because of its painful nature. They hadn't come back to find her mother, even though that might still be an option. She couldn't help being in awe, and not in a good way, at the alternate reality her father had built for himself, in which there was always someone else to blame.

Or it could be that he was right this time, and her mother had somehow lost the capacity to be a parent, the urge to follow other impulses too tempting. She'd written music and sang in a band. She'd sung to Joanna when she was little.

"Okay. I'd like you to give me that information, and we'll leave you alone."

"Very well."

He got up to leave the room and returned only moments later with a thick envelope. Joanna was glad he didn't take much time. She couldn't talk to Rue right now without embarrassing herself.

"Thank you. For what it's worth, I didn't send that guy. I hope they'll catch him soon."

The fact that he didn't deny he'd thought of the possibility, told her everything she already knew.

For a too brief moment, she could have almost fooled herself into thinking there was something about her he was proud of—but he couldn't praise a woman without disrespecting another, soft-spoken and polite as usual.

She'd gotten what she wanted. Joanna clutched the envelope tightly as if someone was going to take it away from her.

She would have liked to go to the hotel room and stay inside with Rue, for drinks, and sex, but there was no time for comfort. They were going to see Rue's parents, and Governor O'Neal afterwards.

Chapter
Nineteen

For a long time, Rue had dreamed about the moment she'd introduce Joanna to her parents. She didn't think that when the occasion arose, it would be under such difficult circumstances. Never mind a serial killer, the lover of the man who abducted her, on the loose.

She was still shaken about what they'd learned, and she wondered if Joanna had managed to process all the implications yet. It looked like Mitchell had known all this time where her mother was. Why not tell Joanna and let her make up her own mind? Joanna had memories of her from the first ten years of her life, and from what Rue knew, they weren't bad. What had changed? Why leave a ten-year-old with a cold-hearted man like Lawrence Mitchell and then stay in touch with him, but not her daughter?

There were numerous possible scenarios. Neither Mitchell nor his ex-wife looked good in any of them.

Rue hoped Joanna wouldn't find her too selfish for wanting to see her own parents as well.

"Joanna! It's so good to finally meet you."

Standing back as her mother hugged a startled Joanna, Rue felt pride in her parents who had always supported and listened to her, during the worst and best times of her life. Even when she had to explain that she was dating a woman who had served time for killing a man, they had listened.

"I'm glad to meet you too."

"Come on in," Rue's dad said, ushering all of them into the living room. "I hope you can stay for dinner."

"Not today, Dad, I'm sorry. We have an appointment this evening...Perhaps we can come back. She didn't want to give them, or herself, false hopes, but being here, Rue couldn't deny how much she'd missed them.

She hoped that Joanna wouldn't feel left out, and that in fact she'd benefit from being around people who behaved like a family should.

They had barely sat down when Joanna got a call.

"I'm so sorry. I have to take that."

She only stepped aside for a couple of minutes, and when she joined them again, her expression signaled both pensive and relieved.

"Tonight's appointment is off," she said. "I guess we have a little more time after all."

Rue hoped the reason was a good one. If the governor thought there was no hurry, what exactly did that mean?

⁂

They stayed for dinner. The officer had conferred with Theo and, after declining the invitation to join them, went home. A relaxed evening with family. Nothing would have revealed the various trials all of them had been through to a casual observer, and that was just fine for Rue. She'd been ready to leave her life behind for Joanna, and she didn't regret her decision—but she was happy to be here.

Despite her anger at Theo for uprooting their lives once again, for the first time, Rue wondered if there was an option for them that didn't mean hiding from the world. She could almost make herself believe that this was normal, just her bringing home a date to meet her parents.

"Let's have some dessert," her father declared and got up to go to the kitchen, her mother following him. For the first time since their visit to Lawrence Mitchell's, they were alone for a moment, one that Rue used to blur out everything that was on her mind.

"I'm so sorry for earlier with your dad. I just couldn't keep my mouth shut."

"That's okay." Joanna smiled softly. "It's kind of nice to have someone in my corner. And I'm glad we're doing this."

"I hope it's not too much. You know there's going to be a nightcap after dessert."

"It's all good. I swear."

"Whatever the reason, he had no right to keep this information from you all those years. You had a right to know."

"Yes, but..." Joanna shrugged. "That's who he is. Frankly, this wasn't even a big surprise." Her body language said otherwise. Rue acknowledged that they'd have to come back to this subject later.

"What did Theo say?"

Before Joanna said anything, Rue realized that this was another painful subject not suitable for pleasant small talk.

"The governor couldn't make the time. And...There's been another murder."

Rue felt a shiver slither down her spine, a touch of cold cutting through the warm comfort of her surroundings. So much for wanting to stay in the city. But Liam Preston had found them anyway.

"I hate them," she said. It might sound childish, but it was still true.

"They can't do this forever. They'll make mistakes."

Her parents returned with coffee and cake, so Rue couldn't ask Joanna what made her so confident.

Perhaps it was just as well that they weren't able to see the governor tonight, Joanna reflected when she sat at the table in the small sitting area of their hotel room while Rue was in the bathroom. She weighed the envelope in her hand.

Part of her couldn't wait to open it. The fact that she hadn't yet was a sign of her growing apprehension as much as the tension that had gripped her tightly.

All of these years, and it could have been this easy? Of course, nothing was ever easy with Lawrence. He had told her not to contact him unless she wasn't gay anymore. She'd gone to see him that other time because of Rue, and today, because it might be the last chance. One might think that having been viciously attacked would make a difference, not that she'd had much hope. She shook her head.

Even knowing him, his attitude was unbelievable. Gay people in the closet, women in "their place." She could easily picture him in some dystopian secret society trying to bring back the "good old times."

But this wasn't about Lawrence, or her relationship with him. This was about the woman who had left them when Joanna was ten years old, never looking back, or perhaps she had, if she accepted help from her former husband. What kind of help? Money to jumpstart her career?

"Why did you leave me there?" she mumbled. She'd had no warning. Mary Mitchell, in her memory, was always kind, warm and soft-spoken. And then she was gone.

She hadn't noticed Rue coming back into the room. She leaned down to gently embrace Joanna.

"You want to open it?"

Wiping a hand over her eyes, Joanna tossed the envelope on the table.

"I can't do this now. Let's deal with Theo and the governor first, and we'll go from there."

She didn't have nightmares that night. Instead, the treacherous dream she'd had often in the weeks after Mary's departure: Her mother holding her, stroking her hair.

Gone.

She woke with the same feeling of being bereft, crying quietly so she wouldn't wake Rue.

Maybe they should have run.

⁂

"How can you take this much time off anyway?"

Vanessa was unfazed by the grumpy greeting she received as she came to get Rue, to go out for breakfast, shopping, Joanna wasn't sure.

She did appreciate the concept. There was nothing much to do for Rue at the police station, and Joanna didn't want her to look at crime scene photos.

Rue and Vanessa left. Joanna headed to the station where Allison and Theo were pouring over the kind of pictures she didn't want on Rue's mind. Some came from a security camera, the images slightly grainy. A man and a woman in non-descript clothes leaving the hotel. The medical examiner's photos of the latest victim were a lot more graphic.

161

Peter Flint, a young bank teller, single, was reported missing by his employer when he hadn't come in to work for several days.

"The motel room where they found him was a mess," Theo said. "Someone tried to clean up, but it looks like they gave up halfway through."

"Maybe we get lucky," Joanna surmised. Neither Theo nor Allison questioned her use of "we," which was both strange and comforting. She needed comfort in all the places she could get it.

"The evidence is still being processed," Allison said. "But it's a motel."

"We got in before housekeeping." Theo remained stubbornly optimistic.

"Grace can't be happy about all this. She likes seduction, and precision, when it comes to the murders. The markers, the cuts, everything had meaning, more than for Short even. Remember what Rue said." She didn't want to remember that Rue had once been in the slasher's captivity and what she endured there. She didn't want to talk about Grace like there was any redeeming quality to the woman, because there wasn't. But they, too, had to be precise, and some things had definitely changed.

"What he does to the bodies, it's different. More brutal, less...refined for a lack of a better word."

Both Theo and Allison looked a little sick at that. It wasn't like she was telling them anything new. They had been at the scene.

"She'll rebel at some point, and that will either help us, or it will get her killed."

"Can't say I feel sorry for her," Allison muttered.

"Neither do I, but we have to take those things into consideration."

"We will," Theo promised.

"Any relation between the victims?"

"Age, relationship status, and the bank where Flint worked, is on the same block as Simmons' workplace. It's possible that they ran into each other, though we don't have evidence they knew each other."

Joanna got up to look at the map on the cork board where the block Theo had indicated was circled in red. Stalking was Grace's thing. To her, it looked like the man by her side simply liked brutal killings, without much preparation or afterthought. She shuddered, all of a sudden wondering if they'd overlooked something. Those hookups Oliver had described...Were they still alive? Did one of them live or work on this same block?

"I need to talk to Denise," she said. "Perhaps the trip to the island wasn't just about me."

"You think he killed someone there?"

"Not necessarily. But he might have stolen someone's information."

"That would be a huge coincidence, don't you think? If he found future victims in the same place?"

"He and Grace might feel differently about the killing method, but sex is a prelude for both of them. Find out more about Maggie and Peter's dating habits, and what options they had close to work and home. See if there are any travels, and I'll get you those names to check from Denise."

There was a flash of irritation on Allison's face, but she nodded. "Let's get on that right away."

Even though time was of the essence, Theo felt like he had to make up for some—okay, a lot of things. He let Joanna make her call and instructed an officer to help her with running names if necessary and gather that information until he and Allison returned.

His partner was annoyed with him, and rightfully so. He decided to take a few minutes to try and explain what the past few years had been like, for this department, and for Joanna.

He wasn't proud of himself knowing everything Joanna had accused him of was true. They needed her to be helpful. If she was, they had a much better case to make to Governor O'Neal, who was somewhat on the fence, but open to ideas. She couldn't condone vigilante justice, but it was within her discretion to acknowledge someone who had turned her life around.

"This isn't good, Theo," Allison told him as soon as they'd sat down in the coffee shop. "She knows her stuff, I'll give you that. If this helps us catch them sooner, great, I'm all for it. But if this goes sideways, it's your career and mine on the line."

"It won't. I promise. I know this isn't ideal, but it's just this one case. After that..."

"Your guilty conscience will let you be?" She shook her head. "I know I've come across as bitchy and jealous in the past few days, but that's not it. Well, perhaps I'm a bit jealous, because it seems to come so easily to her...regardless, I'm afraid you are both trying to re-negotiate the past."

"Lester and Preston are killing people in this city right now."

"Yes, and perhaps we need even more detectives on this case. Joanna Mitchell isn't one."

"The governor could probably help her if she had something to show for, like assisting us with our case. O'Neal and I are working on a solution."

"Working on a solution, you and the governor?" Allison repeated incredulously.

This was the first time he had shared the full extent of the possibilities with anyone. Allison's reaction was pretty much what he'd expected.

"That means what exactly? She's going to get her shield back? Come on. Everyone in the department knows what she did, clean slate or not."

"We all know that first conviction was iffy."

"You say that now, but it seemed that back then, everyone was convinced it was an execution. Joanna didn't get convicted because people felt sorry for a dead serial killer. As you know, there was a whole lot more at stake. Again, I don't want to be the woman bashing another woman on the job, but we're all dealing with the same reality. We all dream of killing those sons of—see, even every swear word that comes to mind is an insult to women. My point is she knew what she was doing."

"I don't think she wants to come back, even if she could. Just this case, I need you to bear with me."

"I guess I have no choice. But thanks for the muffin. I really needed that."

"I knew it would help." He grinned, sobering quickly when his cell phone rang.

"Theo," Joanna said on the other end, "I think we have a hit."

⚭

"No, absolutely not." In spite of what she had promised, Allison Kato wasn't going to have Joanna be present when questioning a possible witness. "In fact, you can go back to your hotel. We're really grateful for your help." She could acknowledge that much. "But this will take a while. I promise we'll let you know if we need you."

She cast a questioning look at Theo who gave her a half-smile. Good enough.

Joanna looked a tad disappointed, but she didn't protest. "Sure. No problem. You know where to find me. I can walk." "Thank you. See you tomorrow."

Chapter Twenty

J oanna hadn't missed the increasing tension between Theo and Allison. She was aware that her presence caused said tension—not that she had much of a choice under the circumstances. They still had to reschedule the meeting with the governor. The fact that the woman wanted to see her in the first place, and that no one thought of arresting her, were good signs.

This might be a breakthrough, and she could focus on her own life again. Still, it was a bit anti-climactic to leave at this moment.

Of the names Denise had given her, one person lived within the red circle: Laura Kingston. Her dates on the island overlapped with Preston's, and she had a bank account with the same bank Peter Flint had worked for.

She might help them get closer to Preston. Joanna fervently hoped that it would be the case, because this kind of unpaid detective work was cruel punishment. She didn't want to think about her old job, didn't want to want it back when there was so much else going on.

At some point, she wouldn't be able to avoid opening that envelope, possibly discover more lies. Of Lawrence, or Mary, she wasn't sure.

Rue remained the only real constant in her life.

"Excuse me? Joanna Mitchell?" a female voice asked, and the next moment, Joanna felt a distinct pressure against her back. That was when she recognized the voice, a reminder of a nightmarish past she was still trying to outrun. It turned out she hadn't been fast enough.

⁂

Joanna's brief hope that the timid, tearful new mother she remembered might not have thought this through vanished quickly.

Anya Decker had a car ready only a few feet away.

"Move," she directed. "Get in there, and no tricks, or I'll shoot you."

In this context, it didn't matter if she was a good or a bad shooter. It was all bad. Joanna obliged, her hands on the wheel. Anya trained the gun on her, though not close enough for Joanna to take it from her without risking both their lives.

"I never imagined you wanted to talk to me." Joanna had thought that with her conviction and prison sentence, Anya had everything she needed. It had been a mistake to forget about her.

"I do now. Drive. And don't try to get anyone's attention," Anya warned. "I'll shoot you, and I'll shoot them."

"You don't want to do that," Joanna tried to reason, but she followed the instructions Decker's widow gave her. Her mind was racing. All this time she'd thought she might be in danger from Grace, or the authorities. It had never occurred to her that Anya Decker thought they had unfinished business. She'd had her say in court that day. "Think of your kid. He needs you."

"His foster parents think otherwise," Anya said bitterly. "Now shut up. I'll tell you where to go."

Her son was in foster care? That was news to Joanna, but of course she hadn't been able to follow the woman's story from prison. Not that she'd wanted to think of a woman who was crying for her dead husband, the serial killer. It made her angry even now.

"I served time." She kept her tone neutral. Despite her emotions for Mrs. Decker, Joanna wasn't suicidal. She had to find a way to talk her out of this. No one would get hurt today. She couldn't risk Anya getting hurt.

"Not enough. You killed him in cold blood."

And I lost everything over it! Joanna didn't yell at her like she wanted for a brief moment. There was no point in provoking her. Besides, it might help if that's what Anya thought of her—an ice-cold killer.

"Where are we going?"

"You'll know when I tell you," Anya snapped.

❧

"Yes, I met this guy on vacation," Laura Kingston confirmed when Theo showed her the photo. "We spent a couple of days together before he had to leave. That's not a crime, is it?" She changed gears when she realized her visitors didn't find her question funny. "Why are you looking for him?"

"Have you ever seen this woman?" Allison asked. "Her name is Grace Lester, but she may have used an alias."

"No, I've never seen her. But you haven't answered my question."

"Do the names Peter Flint or Maggie Simmons mean anything to you?"

"What is this, twenty questions? What's the deal with Liam?"

"Haven't you seen the news?" Theo asked, perplexed. "He's a suspect in three murders and an assault."

"That is...terrible." Her expression was guarded now. "I mean, wow. Between my jobs and school, I don't really have time to follow the news much. Are you sure? We just had a really good time on the island. Maybe you have the wrong guy."

Something sprang to mind. Theo thought of a moment when Joanna had reminded him that victims sometimes withheld information for the fear of judgment, like Christina Danvers had at first. But Kingston wasn't a victim—or had she told the whole truth?

"There was nothing about him that struck you as odd or worrisome?"

She shrugged. "I had a few days off from everything. Lots of sun and alcohol, and a sexy guy was showing interest. It was perfect. No, I didn't think there was something odd about it. Just a vacation flirt."

"Did you make any plans to meet afterwards, since you live in the same city?"

Her answer came with a delay that made Theo curious.

"Um, no, not really. I didn't know that. I assume he has already moved on. Why do you think it's him?"

"The victim of the assault could describe him."

"A woman? Was she raped?"

"No. He walked into a man's office and beat him up."

Laura Kingston listened, shaking her head in disbelief. "I still think you are looking for the wrong guy. Maybe that man was mistaken. It happens, right?"

"Sometimes. Ms. Kingston, if you can think of anything else, please let us know. If there's anything out of the ordinary, please don't hesitate to call 911. It's important."

They walked down the stairs to the front door, and before they reached the lobby, Allison said, "She's lying."

"I know, but about which part?"

"I'd feel better if we kept an eye on her."

"Me too. Let's run this by the D.A."

His phone rang, and he picked it up to find Rue on the other end.

"Please tell me Joanna is with you."

Damn it all to hell.

"Joanna went home a couple of hours ago. Where are you?"

"Still at the hotel with Vanessa," Rue said, the fear in her voice chilling him. "Please, could you come here?"

"I'm on my way," he promised.

⟡

"I thought you moved away after the trial." Joanna still felt shaky after the two shots Anya Decker had fired in the living room of her old home, too close for comfort. That answered one of her questions—she knew how to shoot. She'd made Joanna sit on a rackety chair in the middle of the room. The house had been abandoned for a long time, a thick coat of dust on the floor and every piece of furniture. It smelled moldy.

"I did, for a while. You forced me out of my home. This was my parents' house, remember? We had graffiti on the wall every day."

"People were angry."

"People are stupid. My husband never got a fair trial. They didn't even know if it was him."

"I know. I saw his victims. I spoke to a survivor. She identified him. Anya..."

"Don't say my name." She shook her head with vehemence. Her hand with the gun remained steady. "You took that away from him, the right to a fair trial. Our home. One time, someone threw a rock through the window of the nursery. There were shards in my baby's bed!"

171

Joanna almost agreed with her that they should have let the authorities done their job. Then again, she had crossed lines as well. This was why they were here.

"Mrs. Decker," she tried again, "I'm not sure what you want from me. I know he killed those women. That is the truth. It isn't going to change because it's painful."

Anya stared right at her. "Did he suffer?"

"Not as much as his victims did, no."

"Good," Anya said, something changing in her tone that set off alarm bells for Joanna. "Then I don't have to make this harder than necessary either." She was surprisingly quick raising her arm, but Joanna anticipated her move, ducking the blow. Anya wasn't going to give up, but as long as she didn't pull the trigger, Joanna knew she had an advantage.

Another shot rang out.

⁂

Rue's knees nearly buckled when she heard Joanna's voice on the other end of the call.

"Are you okay? What happened?"

"I'm fine." Joanna didn't sound fine at all. "Could you give me Theo please?"

Rue had no choice but to hand the phone over.

"I understand," he said tersely. "We'll be there in a few minutes. I promise." His tone softened on the last words, doing nothing to disperse Rue's fears.

"I'm coming with you."

"Of course," he said to her relief. "I'll fill you in on the way."

Rue couldn't believe what she heard when they were on the road.

"Anya Decker? I thought..." She didn't have to finish the sentence. They'd all had the same fear when Joanna didn't answer her phone.

"I'm not sure how she even knew Joanna was in town, but apparently, she lost custody of her child and blames her for all of it. She never fully believed that Decker had murdered those women."

"In how much denial can a person be?"

He sighed. "A lot, in her case. Joanna handled herself well."

"Of course she did. But she didn't deserve this."

"I agree."

Rue's heart sank when they arrived at the scene where squad cars and two ambulances were already blocking the street. She saw the woman that had to be Anya Decker being wheeled out on a stretcher, and despite Theo's warnings, all but jumped out of the car.

"She's lying. It's all her fault! She did this!" Decker might be injured, but she hadn't lost her voice. The doors of the ambulance closed after the paramedics got her in, and Rue saw an officer guiding Joanna outside.

She had lied about something. The bruise on the side of the face didn't make it look like she was fine. Rue ran towards her and embraced her, feeling her wince. She couldn't help it. She wasn't sure if it was her, or Joanna shaking, or both of them.

"She tried to shoot herself," Joanna said, drawing a shaky breath. It took Rue a moment to realize she was talking to Theo who had come up behind them. "I tried to stop her."

"We'll figure it all out," he said. "Let's get you checked out first. Rue will go with you, and then I'll need you back at the station."

"Can't this wait?" Rue asked, irritated.

"I need Joanna's statement as soon as possible. Just so we'll get ahead of any possible...complications."

She didn't dare ask what those complications would be. "Let's make sure she's all right first."

~~~

On the bright side, she didn't have a concussion. Joanna had a near blinding headache nonetheless, and she wasn't looking forward to answering any more questions about this latest puzzling and violent detour.

She had no doubts that Anya Decker would want to cast her in the worst possible light. There was something startlingly familiar about that.

"She came up behind me with a gun," she told Allison Kato. "She made me get into the car and drive to her old house where we sat in the living room for a talk."

"All this time, there was no opportunity for you to take the gun?"

"I knew she was desperate, and if I made a mistake, one of us would end up dead."

Allison nodded, giving no indication whether or not she believed Joanna's side of the story.

"What happened next?"

"She wanted to know if Decker had suffered, so I told her the truth. She decided she was going to hit me over the head first, and that's when I saw an opportunity. We fought...She managed to pull the trigger, but fortunately the bullet didn't go where she wanted it to be."

Joanna had no idea what was happening, or why reliving those moments made her lean forward and cry. She had done what she needed to do, watch Anya until the ambulance and the police arrived. She didn't want her to die or try to get away.

Perhaps her father had been wrong about the one thing he didn't seem to hate about her. She didn't feel very strong at the moment. Despite her best efforts, Anya had gotten hurt. She wanted to avoid that, aside from the problems it could cause her.

Rue had to fight off a criminal in a place that was supposed to be safe, where Joanna was supposed to keep her safe.

Mary had decided she didn't want to be a mother anymore.

This was as much as she'd been able to handle. The line had been crossed.

"It's okay," Allison said softly. She'd never spoken to Joanna like that, and it was freaking her out.

"No. None of this is okay."

"Maybe not right now, but this will all be over soon. You'll be able to go home."

She wasn't even sure where that was anymore, except there could be no home without...

Rue walked inside that exact moment.

"Give us a few minutes?" she directed Allison. It wasn't a question, and Allison didn't take it as such.

Chapter
Twenty-One

R ue didn't try to tell her that everything would be all right, and somehow, that was a bigger comfort to Joanna than any reassurances that could end up being false.

"Oh man, this embarrassing," she said, straightening, fairly surprised that no one had walked in on them. After all the police station was a busy place.

"Sure," Rue said, locating a box of tissues that she handed to Joanna. "You got threatened with a gun by the widow of a serial killer and hit over the head. Then you had to keep her from killing herself or you, we don't know for sure, and it's a little much. Yes, by all means, be embarrassed." Her tone was calm and matter-of-fact, devoid of any scorn.

Joanna couldn't help it, she had to laugh. "Smart."

"You know I am. But frankly, this is getting old. What are the odds?"

Joanna still had a headache, and the crying fit hadn't helped, though she had asked herself the same question. Had Anya Decker really prepared her revenge all this time, for the faint chance that she might see Joanna again? That didn't seem to make sense, but what did at the moment?

"I don't know, maybe she snapped after she lost custody. She came back here and started to make plans. Ironically, she made it a lot less likely to get her son back, no matter what story she's telling."

Rue shuddered.

"What?"

"She was yelling and screaming when they brought her out, calling you a liar."

"She said she wanted to make sure I went back to prison. Not that it's likely, but I'm done with people trying to set me up." Joanna touched the side of her head gingerly. "It still hurts, and I'm starving. Let's find Theo and see if we can finally go home."

***

Back at the hotel room, Joanna opted for a quick shower and a change of clothes, hoping she'd be able to scrub the stench of the past off of her. She felt a bit more human when she dressed in jeans and a t-shirt and wound up her hair in a lose bun.

She stared at her reflection in the mirror, the new gray that had appeared in her hair, more lines on her face. Not weak. She had been ambushed and been able to avoid a catastrophe. Anya Decker would have to face the consequences of her actions, as Joanna had.

No, she wasn't weak, but it wasn't up to Lawrence to decide that either. Or Mary. Determined, she walked into the bedroom and took the envelope from the side table, ripped it open and let the content fall onto the table.

Joanna was aware of Rue's startled gaze, but she couldn't go back now.

The papers were a mix of copies of checks, bank statements, and other official documents. They showed a pattern of regular payments Lawrence made to her mother after she had left.

"She took that money." Joanna sat, the sudden drop of energy making her light-headed. "All those years, she took money from him. She was no better."

"We don't know all the reasons yet. Do you want to meet her?"

"I don't know if it's necessary to do that to myself. There's nothing she could say that would make either of us feel better."

"Just to make sure. So, there's no doubt on your side."

"Maybe. But I need food now. I can't think clearly anymore."

"Of course. Let's go have dinner."

Perhaps she was all out of energy to worry, or the wine she was having with dinner helped. In any case, Joanna couldn't be much concerned when Theo called her later and told her what Decker's wife had said in her statement.

"Not that it matters much. She's not much credible."

"Even less than I am," she said, amused.

"If you want to put it that way. I don't think there will be a problem. I just wanted to let you know Governor O'Neal will see you on Saturday. She's inviting us to dinner with her husband. Rue and Vanessa are invited too."

"Wow, fancy. I'm not sure I brought clothes for that."

"Joanna, this is serious. If we play this right, all of this could be over soon."

She remembered that Allison had used a similar phrase.

"I wish," she said. "Vanessa promised me before, and look where we are."

"Vanessa's friends usually help women who need to stay hidden. This was different."

"Because you still had use for me?"

"Because you can still turn this around," he said patiently. "Enjoy the evening and try to relax. I'll talk to you again when you're sober. Say hello to Rue."

"Wait, is there any news about Preston and Lester?"

"There might be soon. See you Saturday."

Allison Kato stayed after hours, something nagging at the back of her mind. She didn't mind the overtime. Her boyfriend was out of town, and her cat only ever greeted her with angry meows these days.

She couldn't stand thinking she'd missed something. The recordings. The picture of Joanna and Preston at the crime scene. He had recorded her, but who had taken the picture? Why did they always come back for Joanna Mitchell?

She went online to search for Laura Kingston, bringing up a social media profile. It was locked, but it turned out she was tagged in someone else's photos, in what looked like a party. Allison clicked through the pictures until she got to the one that made her jaw drop and reach for her cell phone.

Theo's voicemail came on, so she sent him a text before she brought up the picture again. Laura Kingston stood next to Maggie Simmons, the two of them toasting to the person taking the picture.

Laura had lied about not knowing Maggie, for starters.

Why Anya Decker? How could she know that Joanna was in town? Why after all this time?

While Joanna wanted nothing but to enjoy Rue's hands and lips on her body, she couldn't get away from those questions. Rue noticed it too, because she halted and sat up, regret in her expression.

"I'm not really doing a great job, am I?"

"You are. It's not you." Joanna took her hand and held it for a moment. She pulled up the sheet to cover herself. "Anya Decker came to court and showed off her baby. That was her agenda, to make me look bad. Once I was convicted, she lost all interest."

"She might have read up on Short, put two and two together."

"But she couldn't know I was here."

"Grace might."

They shared a look, both of them trying to make sense of these puzzling segments. "True," Joanna said, "and she might be aware of what happened at the trial when she did her homework on me. But she couldn't know that Preston would break her out, or that Anya would come back."

"What if it wasn't her? What if Preston organized all of it while Grace was still locked up? They were mocking you, trying to set you up. Now, all those years later, Anya Decker all of a sudden decides to do the same."

Perhaps she'd been afraid to say it out loud. Now that Rue had, they couldn't turn away from the dire possibilities. Preston, wherever he came from, had known that Grace felt like Joanna had done her wrong, and he dangled revenge in front of her like the proverbial carrot.

"I have to call Theo," she said. "They need to ask Anya about Grace."

"Don't worry. I need just a moment of your time, and then you can get back to sleep."

The soft whisper startled Anya Decker awake.

"There you are," Dr. Lester told her with a smile.

Truth be told, she wasn't a real doctor, but when she caught her reflection in the window, Grace could almost make herself believe. She looked good in the white coat. No one had stopped her.

"I did everything you said," Anya told her.

"That's good. And you didn't tell anyone about me."

"No, why would I?"

"Very good. I hope you hit her hard."

A relieved smile appeared on Anya's face. "As hard as I could."

"That's my girl," Grace said, and with a swift move, placed the pillow over Anya's face, putting her whole weight into the movement until the woman stopped struggling. "You thought we were the same," she said, shaking her head. "That's cute."

When she left the room, Grace heard approaching sirens outside. Things were getting a little hot in this town, but she wasn't ready to leave yet.

She hoped Liam had been successful on his end as well. Perhaps they could celebrate.

❧

"Well, thank God I have an alibi," Joanna said after she laid down the phone. "Anya Decker is dead."

She sounded in shock. She probably was. There was no lost love between her and the woman who wanted her back in prison so badly, a woman who had successfully maintained the illusion that her husband could still be an ordinary, good guy.

Joanna had never wanted her dead, and she was convinced that this murder proved her theory: Grace had somehow forged a connection with Decker's widow and used her as a pawn.

Theo had promised to come by to get her up to date. She was on pins and needles until he managed, around midnight. He looked ragged, though Joanna had to remind herself that her appearance probably wasn't much better. This wasn't a typical murder case. Grace and her new lover had unleashed Armageddon on the city, or so it felt. All because of Joanna? She might be overestimating herself. Both Grace and Liam were psychopaths. They did whatever they pleased, with or without an explanation attached. This went far beyond her.

"Security footage shows a doctor going into her room that no one recognizes. The intruder smothers her with a pillow and walks right out. We must have missed her by minutes."

He cast a look at the papers still on the side table, but when Joanna didn't elaborate, he didn't ask.

"In all of this, we never had a chance to talk about the woman who was at the inn, Kingston? How did that go?"

"Allison found something, a photo online that shows her with one of the witnesses. I was going to meet her when you called and the fact that Anya might be able to lead us to Grace took priority..." He raked a hand through his hair. "She sent me a message that we have to check on Kingston."

"And did you?"

"Joanna, when I came to the station, she wasn't there anymore. I called Laura Kingston, she hasn't heard from Allison. We can't find her."

Joanna's hand went to her mouth. She knew exactly what that meant, her vision graying out when her mind went back to the crime scene photos.

"You don't think...?"

Of course, that was what he was thinking, what they were all thinking.

"She's not in her apartment. Her car is missing. We have a BOLO out already."

"We'll find her," Joanna promised him without a second of hesitation. Because she knew they would. Because she knew this was the ultimate challenge Grace had issued to her, and she wouldn't let her win.

Chapter Twenty-Two

A lison Kato came to in a panic, her heart beating painfully hard against her chest. The moments after she'd left the department remained fuzzy in her memory, but she knew one thing without a doubt: she was in trouble.

Possibly, fatal trouble.

She was sitting upright on the floor of what looked like an apartment, her hands tied behind her back, around the column separating kitchen and living space. She couldn't make out any sounds. That meant she was alone. For now. Not that it helped her much: The cuffs around her wrists were tight, forcing her back in a straight position. At the moment, the metal cutting into her skin was the only source of pain. Allison wasn't kidding herself. She had seen the crime scenes, Maggie Simmons, Peter Flint.

The killers had been in a frenzy, and it wouldn't really make a difference to her if Grace Lester was more or less uncomfortable with the setting. She wouldn't make any attempt to hold him back.

History repeated itself.

She remembered every single moment of the search for Rue, time running out.

But Rue had been lucky, because Joanna Mitchell was willing to risk everything for her.

Maybe I should have been nicer to her.

A sob rose in her throat, not because she thought Joanna didn't care, but because the odds didn't look good for her. They couldn't always be so lucky.

Maggie and Peter sure hadn't been. She didn't even know if Theo had received her message. Allison let the tears fall, determined to get them out of her system.

She wasn't going down without a fight.

⚬

Laura Kingston had joined Theo at the station without protest when he told her that a woman had been murdered tonight, and another was missing.

"I can talk to her," Joanna offered. "It will be recorded."

He looked doubtful but didn't put up a fight.

"You are needed elsewhere."

"Okay. Be careful," he warned her.

"Of course. Good luck. Ms. Kingston, come with me please," she instructed the pale woman. She opened the door to the interview room and waited for Laura Kingston to sit. Joanna closed the door and sat across from her. "As you can see, it's very busy right now. If you could tell me everything you know about Liam, when you first met him, and the interactions you had?"

Laura looked at her in confusion.

"I know you!"

Now, this could go either way.

"On the island, at the inn! Why are you here? Why are they questioning me about Liam?"

"He hurt a lot of people." Even though they were alone in the room, Joanna lowered her voice. "Did he hurt you?"

"No." Laura's denial was swift and believable. Her issue lay probably elsewhere, something Joanna could relate to. Like Joanna, Laura was the one who got away. "This is just so...It's so hard to believe. We had a good time together. He told me to find him on this dating app, and that we could get together with his girlfriend, and she didn't mind..."

"You looked him up online?" Joanna was halfway out of her chair.

"Yes, I thought that was why the detective asked me to come back?"

"What kind of app? Was Maggie on it too?"

"Yes, we both were. I just couldn't believe...I'm so sorry." She was crying in earnest now. "If it's true what they said about him, if he killed those people, he might have done it before. And because I slept with him, I was somehow...tainted? I'm so disgusted with myself right now."

"You couldn't know," Joanna reasoned. "We'll figure it out. I need to see that app right now."

With shaking hands, Laura took out her phone. She went online, found the site of the dating app and logged into her account.

"Check for a Peter Flint too."

"He's here," Laura said after a few seconds. "But I swear I never talked to him. This is Liam."

Joanna took the phone from her, looking at the photograph of a man she knew. A killer. Who might have gone after Allison Kato.

"Okay, Laura, please stay here. I have to make some calls."

She needed Theo or anyone who could contact the D.A. for warrants on Preston's account. They had to come up with some sort of personal information, an address, a real phone number...a chance to locate him.

No, Joanna couldn't stay away. It didn't seem to be such a bad thing at the moment.

⁂

Allison wasn't alone any longer. They stood in a corner, talking quietly to each other, every once in a while regarding her like one would a bug under a microscope—moments before they'd rip off a leg. She was running out of time, and all she could think of were the gruesome details from the murders she'd worked on with Theo. The recent ones were enough to turn her stomach.

Lester and Short had had their own ritual, and it included specifics she didn't want to think about either. Preston just made everything so much worse. She almost hoped she'd faint, but no such luck.

Allison had faced danger at times in her career, but nothing like this. She stiffened when Preston turned abruptly and walked over to her. She could see the smile forming on Grace's face. By now, Theo must have gotten her message, but would talking to Kingston make a difference? Would it be soon enough?

Preston crouched in front of her, grinning. "Detective Kato," he said. "Welcome to your nightmare."

"You're probably wondering, why you?" Grace added. "It's true, you're not all that important in the big scheme of things, but everyone is watching Joanna's friends now. Too dangerous for us."

"They'll figure it out," Allison shot back. Her mouth was dry, adding to the impression that she could barely breathe.

"Yeah, maybe, but I'm afraid it will be too late. This is really cool, isn't it? No one thought that you were even on our radar. And they'll also be busy with Anya."

"That was smart." Perhaps flattery would buy her some time. Allison wasn't sure, but at this point, she had to try anything.

"Oh yes, I know." Grace smiled as if pleased with the praise. She probably was. She knew that they had time. "Silly woman, she thought we had so much in common. She was also a whiner, so I think we can all agree everyone's better off with this solution. What about you, Allison? How's your tolerance for pain?"

"What happened to offering something to your victims that was too good to refuse?"

Grace shrugged. "You're not interesting or young enough. But I can't get to little Rue at the moment, and you're the next best thing. Sorry."

The slap to her face came out of nowhere, making her teeth rattle. She couldn't hold back the yelp.

But looking at the object Preston was weighing in his hands, Allison went quiet.

If there was ever a moment to pass out, it was now.

"This is all my fault," Theo said angrily. "We've dealt with her before. We knew she has no boundaries. Allison warned me, and now she's paying for it."

"Allison's savvy," Joanna reminded him. "And whatever happens, it's not your fault." It was lip service at this point, she knew. If Short had murdered Rue, she wouldn't have been able to live with herself. And Theo was aware of that too, so nothing she said could offer him real comfort as they waited for the warrant.

Rue sat in the corner, quiet and withdrawn. Joanna felt sorry she had to relive her nightmare, but there was no way she could have left her at the hotel alone. Here at the station was still the safest place. "We're going to get an address on Preston. We must be close, otherwise they wouldn't have moved so fast," she tried again.

"If it's not too late," Theo said darkly.

"Anya Decker must have known quite a bit about them if they considered her a loose end," Rue spoke up. "If she didn't go back to stay in her house while she was stalking Joanna, where was she living? Did she have any family in town? Did anyone claim the body?"

She sounded almost frantic, Joanna realized with a start, too much like Joanna herself. It was wrong. Neither of them should be here, but Grace, and from the grave, a couple of other serial killers left them no choice. Decker, Short, Grace, and Liam Preston. So many connections, it was easy to ignore the forest for the trees.

In his dating profile, Preston had listed true crime stories as one of his interests. That asshole.

"Maybe that's not the right question. What happened to Violet Short?"

"She's still in her house," Theo said. "That's all a bunch of nothing."

"Preston studied Grace, and the murders before he got her out. He wanted something to present to her."

"How is this helping?"

They all jumped when Theo's phone rang.

"All right," he said after listening to the caller for a couple of minutes. "Let's do this."

Joanna hadn't been so far off. The phone number Preston had listed belonged to Edward Short's mother Violet, a detail

Grace might appreciate. But the address Liam Preston had listed with his account on the dating app was an unfamiliar one.

"You two stay here. I'll let you know as soon as I can."

***

"I think I'm going to throw up," Rue confessed when they were alone in the room. The frantic activity around them made her dizzy, and fear had a tight hold on her.

"No one's going to judge you for that."

She could tell Joanna was restless, on the verge of...something. Something stupid, or dangerous. Rue didn't want to know.

"There's nothing you can do for her." *Like you did for me* remained unspoken. "They'll find her." One way or another. She didn't say that out loud either.

"I know. It's been...tough," Joanna admitted. "We still don't know what the governor's deal is. They want me here for something, but whenever there's movement, they slam the door in my face." She sighed. "Not that I'm complaining right now. Of course, it's all because of Grace. I thought she wanted to get back at me, but I'm starting to feel like that's megalomaniacal. She just wants to wreak havoc and found the right guy for it."

"We'll see this through," Rue said with a whole lot more confidence than she felt at the moment. So much violence and death. How could a person ever overcome that?

***

Grace could see it in his gaze. He wanted to go in for the kill. Any other time, she wouldn't mind, but this might be her last chance to have her ultimate showdown with Joanna.

She didn't want Allison Kato dead for that. Frankly, she was tired of the sloppy execution. Liam had made it look like he admired her, yet he wanted to control everything. Not that he had much of it, self-control.

"No," she said sharply when he approached Kato again.

"No?" He turned to her with a grin that she had found charming when she realized the prison guard had turned out to be her rescuer. Now, Grace was annoyed with him. At least Edward was the devil she knew. "Did you really just say that?"

She could sense that Allison was holding her breath. False hopes, sweetie, she thought. It doesn't mean that I want to spare you.

"What if I did? We have to wait. Joanna will find her way here, somehow."

"What if she doesn't? She's not clairvoyant." For someone how liked to butcher his victims, Liam used big words sometimes. "I understand you wanted to rattle her a little, but we don't need her."

"I thought you understood!" Grace's voice rose to a higher pitch. "The lengths you went to in order to break me out, and you're still too stupid to understand? I hate you."

She would have said more if he hadn't slapped her in the face, hard enough to make her stumble.

"Remember who's calling the shots here? Huh?"

With him in her personal space, Grace should have sensed the danger, but she was too pissed for self-preservation. "I thought you were smarter than that, but you're just another loser like—"

She could hear Allison sob, wondering if she had overestimated herself—or Joanna Mitchell. She might not get her revenge after all. Mediocre men would always win.

Chapter
Twenty-Three

T he SWAT team breached the entrance of the apartment, and Theo ran inside, nearly slipping in a puddle of blood on the shiny hardwood floor. His heart skipped a beat as he fell to his knees next to Allison. Her wrists were still fastened with cuffs around the column, the keys tauntingly left behind on the kitchen counter. She was slumped forward, but flinched when he touched her shoulder gently, his fingers coming away wet.

"It's okay. You're safe now. We got you."

From every room, members of the SWAT team returned, announcing that the place was clear.

They were gone. He wanted them to pay for what they had done to Allison, make it painful, but that would have to wait. The paramedics brought in a stretcher, and he removed the cuffs with gloved hands. They put her on the stretcher, the pained whimpers branded on his mind.

"I want this place searched from top to bottom," he advised an officer. What he really wanted to do was what Joanna had done. Given how he had reacted back then, Theo wasn't sure if that would make him a hypocrite or merely human.

"They found Allison," Joanna said, and after a small pause. "She has some injuries, but she'll be okay."

Some injuries. Rue turned that over in her mind, wondering how they had talked about her after finding her in the place where Edward Short had held her. Some injuries. She'd survived with some cuts and shallow stab wounds, nothing life-threatening, but the invisible scars remained with her forever. She started to cry, barely getting the words out.

"That's good, right? So, we...We can go to the hotel?"

"I don't know, maybe we should wait." Joanna sounded worried.

"Why?"

"They left her."

To die, Rue supplied in her mind. "This is never going to end, is it?"

"It has to. At some point, they'll have nowhere left to go."

"Grace and Edward got away with it for eleven years. What makes you think they won't?"

Joanna had no answer for her. "Maybe you're right," she relented. "There's nothing much we can do here."

Joanna sent Theo a text, with get well wishes for Allison and to ask him to bring her up to date whenever he was ready. In another time, she would have gone to the hospital, but she knew the waiting room would already be filled with cops. It wasn't her tribe any longer. She had to come to terms with the fact that she'd been called here for one reason only, and even that seemed superfluous now.

Grace had wanted to toy with her, and she'd had her day. They'd do everything to keep the investigators off balance, make them guess and change course again. She shuddered at the thought that leaving Allison alive was nothing but random.

Or was it?

When they sat in the car, she said, "I'd like to check in with Theo one more time."

Rue shrugged.

A moment later, she had him on the phone. "Hey, I'm sorry to bother you, but is there anything new? You know why they left? Someone interrupted them, or somebody tipped them off?"

"Slow down a second, Joanna. This was well planned out. The store downstairs was closed, and the other two apartments were empty. They made sure no one would hear anything."

Screams, she thought. "Okay, but don't you think...?"

"It's strange that they left her alive? Allison couldn't talk much, but she said they had a fight. That's why there was so much blood. It looks like he's getting tired of her."

Something about that sentence bothered her, but Joanna acknowledged this probably wasn't the time to address the subject. No one in their right mind could feel sorry for Grace. She hadn't fallen into an age-old societal trap. She had chosen to be with a serial killer, all the way, twice.

"That's good news, then, right? He's the sloppy one, she's smart, but if they have a falling-out..."

"It looks that way." Theo sounded exhausted. "Let's hope it will work in our favor."

This time, she knew she wasn't included, and Joanna was strangely okay with that.

"Okay. Thanks. We'll talk tomorrow. Rue and I are going to the hotel now."

"Good idea. Get some rest."

If only.

⁂

"It was scary. I thought he was going to kill her first, and then me. But he just dragged her out of the room, and then they were gone."

With her face cleaned up and her bloody clothes replaced with a hospital gown, Allison looked a lot better though the traces of her ordeal were obvious. Theo hadn't completely lost the impulse to hurt somebody, specifically Lester and Preston. It was a bit easier to control now that they could have this calm conversation. He couldn't help wondering if at some point, he, too, would feel like he had to do more than the powers given to him by the law allowed him.

It didn't seem enough. It hadn't been enough for Joanna. While each of them understood what it was like, they had treated her like a shield to hide behind, let her take the fall by herself.

"I'm not sure what to make of that face of yours," Allison said. "No news yet?"

"I'm sorry, no. I was just thinking how much I'd like to shoot that son of a bitch."

"I get the sentiment, believe me." She shifted, pain making the color drain from her face. "Now what? You're going to give Joanna a badge? Budget's tight, and I'll be out of commission for a while."

He couldn't tell if she was serious or not, about Joanna anyway.

"She was a great help, but I'll want my partner back eventually."

For the first time since he'd found her, Theo saw her smile.

⁂

The next morning, Joanna changed her mind and decided to go and see Allison at the hospital. While she was beyond relief about the outcome, "lucky" once more, Rue couldn't bring herself to join her. She had spent most of the morning in bed, sleeping on and off, mostly to keep herself from drowning in worst-case scenarios. Eventually she took a shower and got dressed.

Joanna was safe. She'd sent a message that she would be back around early afternoon. Rue thought that she could manage a quick breakfast before that.

She wondered if everyone would agree that Joanna had paid her dues. She helped to draw Grace out and had offered her ideas. If they expected more of her, she and Rue would likely be stuck here until the serial killer duo was behind bars, not an uplifting prospect. Regardless of any expectations from former colleagues, Joanna might consider it her duty to stay until arrests were made, despite the lack of a paycheck or otherwise acknowledgments.

Rue missed their simpler life on the island. She was getting tired or sitting around or being babysat by Vanessa. If only the governor would confirm they'd be free to come and go as they pleased.

Rue wanted to *go*.

After getting dressed, she went downstairs and decided on a pastry and coffee from the shop across the street rather than the buffet. She paid for both and brought them back to the hotel room, juggling her purchases in one hand as she opened the door with the other.

Rue put coffee and the small bag on the side table, distantly noting her hand was sticky. Had to be the powdered sugar...She looked down at her hand and gasped at the red smear. She wondered if she was still dreaming, had in fact never gotten out of bed...On weak knees she walked further into the room. More blood on the carpet.

"Hello Rue. It's so nice to finally meet you in person. I trust you not to do anything stupid."

Stupid? Rue didn't think she was able to do anything, frozen to the point of paralyzed, her heart beating in her throat.

The sight in front of her was almost enough to generate pity, if not sympathy, hadn't she known who Grace Lester was, and the hell she'd unleashed. It was because of her that Short had wanted to torture and kill Rue. He'd even set up video, so he'd have something to present to her.

Grace didn't look like the ruthless killer she was. Her face and hands were bloodied, her clothes stained. Yet, she was training a gun on Rue in a surprisingly stable grip.

"What do you want?" Rue managed to get out.

"I need you to help me," Grace hissed.

The situation, and her request, were so absurd Rue felt laughter bubbling up in her throat. Maybe she was going insane, hallucinating the whole thing.

"Me? Help you? Why would I do that?"

"Because I have a gun, stupid!"

Rue couldn't argue with that fact, though she hoped she'd have her chance to get back at her. Who was Grace calling stupid anyway? She'd gotten in bed with a serial killer and not imagined that he might turn on her? Like Edward Short had? He'd gotten rid of her when he left her behind in prison. Yet she'd teamed up with another monster. Maybe it was too early for that given her own predicament, but Rue did feel something akin to pity.

"Okay. I can see that," she said, slowly raising her hands. "What do you want me to do? You need meds, water? A coffee? I bought breakfast." She could see the woman's eyes narrow as Grace was probably trying to figure out if Rue was taunting her.

Maybe she was, but certainly not on purpose. She simply blurted out the first things that came to mind.

"He's gone mad," Grace said, a hint of regret to her voice.

"Maybe he always was. Did you consider that?"

"You might be right," Grace agreed to Rue's surprise. "But it wasn't like I had a lot of options, was it? When the detective came to see me about Joanna's dad, I had no idea what was going on. Liam was a real gentleman at first."

Listening to her delusions was almost enough for Rue to ignore the gun. She wanted to shake her, but she was aware that she'd achieve nothing except getting herself killed. Grace was weakened. Perhaps she'd pass out, and then Rue could take the gun from her and call 911...

"He did this to you? Why don't we call the police and let them know? Isn't going back to prison better than your current situation?"

Grace shook her head. "That's what they make us do, hide away, cower in fear. I swore to myself I'd never do that."

Yet you're here, hiding from him and dragging me into your mess, Rue thought angrily.

"It's not that simple. You need to step up so he can't hurt anyone else."

She knew she'd chosen the wrong thing to say when Grace's fingers tightened around the gun. Rue held her breath until her vision started to waver.

"Or I could just shut you up!"

"Why don't we start by getting you cleaned up a bit? You can have my breakfast if you want. I meant that."

"There's no time for any of this," Grace said darkly.

"Why is that?"

"Because he's coming here. Call Joanna. I want to talk to her before it's all over."

~~~

After the hospital visit, Joanna had joined Theo at the station where she could witness more of the mystery being unraveled: Liam Preston had spent considerable time online looking for information on the crimes of serial killers, Grace Lester and Edward Short in particular. Once they'd had all the information that the earlier warrant had produced, a pattern emerged:

He had researched Grace and Edward, Joanna, and everyone else involved. He also had a wealth of personal information on one particular prison guard. He'd been on shift when Preston broke out Grace, signing off on the papers.

Theo was about to leave with a couple of officers to bring him in when Joanna's cell phone rang.

"It's Rue. I think I'll go and meet her for lunch."

"Yeah, you do that."

He saw her pale and immediately knew another crisis was unfolding, even before Joanna said,

"Grace! What the hell are you doing with Rue's phone?"

Chapter Twenty-Four

S omething softened in Grace's expression when she spoke to Joanna. Sympathy? Pity? Jealousy? Rue didn't have the time to sort through any of those emotions. Granted, any of them was better than the fear Grace might end the call and shoot her, put an end to some sort of twisted love triangle.

"You come here. You don't tell anyone, and you help me. You get me out of this, and I'll leave little Rue alone. How does that sound?"

Rue bristled at the nickname though there wasn't much she could do about it. How did Grace figure this would work? She and Joanna would run away together? That was laughable. She'd break into hysterical laughter at any moment. It was all too grotesque.

"All right, babe, I'll see you soon. I missed you so much," Grace whispered. Was there a trace of emotion in her voice? Rue wasn't going to be fooled. A psychopath with that much blood on her hands wasn't capable of affection. In that moment, Rue realized that none of it had anything to do with her. It never had. Short had abducted her, maybe would have even tried to get the video to Grace, but Rue was never the one Grace wanted.

Joanna was.

"No!" she cried. "Don't come here! She's going to kill you!"

"Shut up!" Grace yelled back at her, throwing the cell phone at Rue with surprising force. It hit her shoulder and cluttered to the floor.

"I understand it now," Rue said, amazed at how calm her voice sounded. "That's why you let Allison live. And you're going to let me live."

"Don't count on it."

"Why do you hate Joanna so much?"

Grace stared her right in the eye, reaching up to touch the bruise on her face that still hadn't stopped bleeding.

"Because she hurt me more than this," she said. "And now she's going to pay."

Both of them froze at the sound of the door opening and being shut softly.

Rue closed her eyes, channeling Zach's voice in her mind. He'd always talked her through her doubts. One of those times she'd been sitting on the bench, leaning against the ropes crying, convinced she'd never overcome the mindset of feeling helpless and hopeless, destined to be prey.

She wasn't stupid. She wasn't little Rue. She refused to be prey.

❧

"You come with me, and you'll do what I say," Theo warned her.

Joanna wasn't going to argue. She knew this was their best bet, to save Rue, to get Grace back behind bars. She was fairly certain that Preston couldn't survive on his own for long. He didn't have her skills and intelligence.

"Don't worry," she said curtly. *If anyone knows the stakes, it's me.*

"I'll gladly come to your wedding," Theo said as they headed to his car. "After that, I need you both to be out of my hair. I'm serious."

"Deal," Joanna said, trying hard to push the worst-case scenarios out of her head.

Rue would be okay, because they all knew it was Joanna that Grace wanted.

That idea hadn't been megalomaniac after all.

This was what it all came down to, a one-night stand gone wrong.

"Jesus," she said out loud. "You were right all along."

"We'll bring her in, and you'll be free."

They weren't there yet, Joanna thought.

❦

It hadn't been hard to follow Grace or anticipate her movements. His research had made her predictable to him, if it hadn't been for her constant talk about Joanna Mitchell. He couldn't understand what was so special about her, but then again, Grace had lost her appeal too when she revealed herself to be a controlling bitch. He was done with all of them. He needed Grace to be gone.

"Little Rue" as Grace liked to call her, was a bit of a bonus, or so he had thought.

Liam didn't expect her to turn into a banshee the moment he walked into the room.

❦

For Joanna, it came down to the basic truth everyone kept reminding her of, the truth she'd tried to deny for so long: She wasn't a cop any longer. That meant she didn't answer to anyone, certainly not Theo. Whatever he and the governor could do for her meant nothing if Rue died in that hotel room.

The police had evacuated the floor where the room was located, created a perimeter and secured the exits. Joanna joined Theo in the area where the SWAT team stood at the ready a few feet away from the door. She was only half-listening to them discuss the next steps.

Grace and Preston seemed to fancy themselves to be a meaner kind of Bonnie and Clyde. They didn't care who was hurt, who died, as long as they got the headlines, the last laugh.

But there was something Grace wanted and giving it to her might be the only chance to get Rue out of this alive.

Joanna knew what she had to do. It was so obvious that she moved without thinking, her hand already on the door handle when she heard Theo's angry shout.

"Joanna! Wait!"

Ignoring him, she slipped inside the room.

The scene that presented itself to Joanna didn't make sense, at all, though she didn't care, grateful beyond measure that Rue was alive, victorious in fact, standing over Preston who was whimpering and writhing on the floor. It was glorious, though not quite the happy ending she'd hoped for, not yet.

Grace, cowering next to an armchair, still clutched a gun in her hands.

"Get him out of here!" she screeched.

"Yes, we will. All in good time. Let Rue go first."

Grace pointed the gun at Joanna, then back at Rue. "I don't want to see him any longer," she yelled. "Get him out!"

"We can handle this between us, right?" Joanna knew it was only a matter of time before the tactical team would breach the door.

"What are you doing here?" Preston spat at Joanna. "You're going to kill me too?"

"Oh no," she said, holding Rue's gaze. "No one's going to get killed. Right, Grace?" *Because the cops will toss your asses back into prison not long from now.* Joanna knew they couldn't trust her or him.

Rue had been holding her own from the looks of it, but he wasn't that badly injured—and Grace might shift gears, and loyalties, any moment.

"We need to talk," Grace said.

"I agree. We don't need Rue for that. This is between me and you."

The anger in Rue's expression was unmistakable, even though it barely masked the naked fear.

"I need a moment with Grace. Please, go."

She'd have a lot to make up for later, but Joanna could tell that for Grace, it worked. She wasn't sure if this could end well for any of them, with both Grace and Preston knowing that they had nowhere to go. She had to take the risk. This was her final debt to pay. Maybe Theo was right, and afterwards, she could be free.

"Yes, leave us alone!"

"I saved your ass," Rue snapped at Grace. "We had a deal!"

"Deal's off, now go, or do you want to find out how many bullets I have left?"

"Go!"

Rue flinched, but she obeyed.

"You brought cuffs?" Grace asked. She tried to sound nonchalant, but Joanna could tell she was fading, in a lot of pain. Good.

"These." She held up the zip ties and bent down to fasten Preston's wrists behind his back. One problem at a time. She could only hope.

"You're insane," he hissed. "This is what she wants."

"Okay, Grace. You'll be okay, I promise. We can get out of here now, but first, you have to give me the gun."

Grace shook her head.

"They have surrounded the place."

"Then there's nowhere to go for either one of us."

"There is. You'll be able to tell your story. He didn't ask you, did he? He came to get you out, and you had to do as he said."

Joanna could swear Preston scoffed at that.

"That is true," Grace said, sounding sad. "None of these bastards ever listened to me."

"I'm listening to you now. Do you hear that, Grace? I'm listening," Joanna said, taking a tentative step closer. "I've always given you the benefit of the doubt, haven't I?"

She was aware of Grace following her every movement.

"I might not understand what you're doing, but I want to. I've told you that before."

"And I've told you before we are the same. Hunters."

Abruptly, Grace started to laugh for almost a minute, until her laughs turned into sobs.

Joanna wasn't sure she'd ever been this disturbed in her life.

"It wasn't true. I didn't kill *with* them. I killed for them, and look where it got me!"

"I'm sorry, Grace. I'm really sorry."

Joanna held out a hand, and so slowly it was nerve-wracking, Grace gave her the gun before she stumbled forward, holding on to Joanna for dear life.

I'm not sorry about this, she thought, reaching for that second pair of zip ties.

It was in that split-second that Grace seemed to have a change of heart and reached for the gun. Joanna, who had half anticipated that action, fought her. A shot rang out, deafening in the confines of the room. She didn't see, only heard the tactical team rush in, instinctively taking a step sideways. Another shot was fired, but neither Joanna nor Grace had pulled the trigger.

Grace, who had cried on her shoulder seconds before, stumbled, looking stunned. She collapsed on the floor.

Joanna realized that when she'd moved aside, she had given the team a clear shot to take out the killer. All of a sudden, many more people were in the room.

She heard someone say, "You can't go in there. Ma'am!" and then Rue was in her arms.

"Joanna!" It wasn't until Rue's shocked exclamation that she noticed the blood on her sleeve and the side of her shirt. Grace's blood.

"It's not mine. I'm okay."

"Thank God." Rue looked ready to keel over, so Joanna pulled her close again, just to be safe, and because she needed the contact more than anything.

"It's over," she whispered. "This time, it's over for real."

Chapter
Twenty-Five

I n the days leading up to the meeting with Governor O'Neal, Joanna and Rue hadn't left their new hotel room much. They had moved to a different hotel altogether, unwilling to stay in the place where Rue had fought Preston to the point her knuckles were still bruised, and where Grace Lester had died.

All of it felt unreal, yet Joanna was well aware of the gravity of their circumstances. That, and their incredible luck for apparently having nine lives between them.

"Don't worry. She's not going to have you arrested now," Rue said behind her, leaning down to kiss her neck.

"I hope not. She can't possibly ask more from either one of us."

"Before we go home, what are you going to do about...?"

She didn't need to say any more.

"I don't know. Let's take it one day at a time?"

"Of course," Rue said. "Ready?"

"As ready as I'll ever be. Let's do this."

Joanna had little time to be impressed with the fact that Governor O'Neal had sent a driver, or the sprawling mansion where the dinner took place.

Vanessa, overdressed as usual, was waiting with Theo in front of the massive staircase.

"I didn't know we were going to the opera," Joanna muttered, making Rue laugh.

She couldn't imagine that this would turn out to be any worse than anything they'd been through before—but she was nervous. It might have to do with the lingering tension, her worry for Rue, the shocking moments when she'd had Grace's blood all over her. What a thin line it was. She doubted anyone would question the person who had fired the shot that killed Grace.

It wasn't Vanessa's job any longer to put those pieces together. All of them could move on now. That's what she hoped, at least.

Governor O' Neal greeted her with a firm handshake.

"I'm glad we could finally make this happen," she said. "Ms. Mitchell, welcome."

"Thank you for having us."

"I think this is overdue. I'd like us to start with appetizers and cocktails, but before that, I'd like to talk to you alone for a moment."

Rue looked startled.

"Yes, of course."

Joanna didn't assume that the Secret Service would be ready to detain her, if that hadn't happened before. She wasn't sure she was completely comfortable with it either, but this was the governor. She wasn't really in a position to say no, so she followed her up the stairs and into a huge office space.

"Please, sit," Governor O'Neal gestured to a sitting area by the window. She sat in the armchair on the other side of the table. Joanna waited, on the edge of her seat. The silence became too uncomfortable, and she said, "I appreciate you seeing me. This must be difficult for you." After hesitating for a heartbeat, she added, "I'm so sorry about Faith." O'Neal and Marian Rickers, Faith's aunt, had been close. Having influential friends had not made a difference to the loved ones of Decker's victims. It might make a difference for Joanna.

"Thank you. Then you probably know that Marian contacted me on behalf of your former partner. I've had a lot of conversations with both of them, and Ms. Vanessa Young, and I've looked into my options."

Joanna wasn't sure what she expected. Remorse? Joanna was glad that this time, thanks to Rue, and thanks to the SWAT team, she didn't have to pull the trigger. She was aware that didn't make her earlier actions go away, and like Vanessa had been, the governor was bound by the law.

"What you did, while many of us certainly thought about doing, didn't bring Faith back. Or the others."

"I understand."

"Ms. Young explained to me why she helped arrange things for you the way she did, and I can see how that made sense to all of you at the time. I wish you could have come to me first, but this is where we are now."

"You were just reelected." Joanna refrained from the impulse to slap her hand against her mouth. Perhaps she should be a bit more...humble?

"This has been messier than any of us could wish for, but Grace Lester and Liam Preston are no longer a threat. You all helped a great deal with that, and I don't see how it would serve anyone to punish you more than you've already been punished. So, I believe a pardon is the best solution here."

Joanna sat, her jaw dropping. So many times, people had told her that it was over, that she could move on.

"That would mean…"

"You'd be free to come and go as you please. You don't have to hide away."

"This is…I don't know what to say."

"A simple thank you would suffice," Governor O'Neal said good-naturedly. "And maybe one to your friends, because they worked hard to convince me."

"I won't forget that."

"Good. Then I think it's time we join them."

O'Neal got to her feet. When she shook Joanna's hand, her eyes were haunted.

"There is really nothing that can console those families, but they'll be glad to know that nightmare is over. I hope you can find some peace."

"Thank you. I'll do my best."

She'd been handed an important missing piece, but it wasn't the last one.

After leaving the governor's mansion, they had celebrated some more with Vanessa and Theo. They'd talked about the wedding. Back at the hotel, they made love. Deeply relaxed the way she could only get with Rue's full attention on her, Joanna had fallen asleep. She woke still in a state somewhere between happiness and tears, disbelief and hope. But they'd made it this far. They were finally safe. She got up to take the envelope out of the drawer once more.

Even though she'd tried her best to do it quietly, Rue woke.

"Hey. You're sure you want to do this now?"

The sun was just starting to rise, a ray of light coming in through the curtains they hadn't closed completely, too much in a hurry.

"If I don't, I might not have the guts later. Better to get it over with, right?"

She clicked on the numbers and sat back down, after three rings hearing the voice she'd missed for so many years.

"Hello?"

After all the demons were gone from her life, Joanna had no more excuses. There was nothing more urgent. She realized she'd been drifting when she heard the impatient sounding question.

"Who's there?"

"Mom?" she said, and the world vanished beneath a blurry veil.

About the Author

B arbara Winkes writes sapphic crime drama and Christmas romance. She loves writing characters who get the job done, whether it's stopping a predator or saving cherished traditions—while still making time for love. She lives with her wife in Quebec City.

barbarawinkes.com

Also by Barbara Winkes

Luce Allen Mysteries
In Harm's Way
Under Pressure

The Crossing Lines Trilogy
Undercover
Redemption
Vengeance

The Connected Series
Promised to the Queen
Drawn to the Enemy
Tempted by the Protector
Saved by the Heiress

Carpenter/Harding
Indiscretions
Insinuations
Incisions
Intrusions

BARBARA WINKES

Initiations
Intentions
Infatuations
Impressions
Implications
Infractions
Incidents
Illusions

Kelli & Merin Romantic Suspense
Thunder
Rain

Lord and Burton
Clean Slate

Standalone
The Amnesia Project